Drowning at the Diner

NIGHTMARE ARIZONA
PARANORMAL COZY MYSTERIES

BETH DOLGNER

Drowning at the Diner

Nightmare, Arizona Paranormal Cozy Mysteries, Book Two

© 2023 Beth Dolgner

ISBN-13: 978-1-958587-08-9

Drowning at the Diner is a work of fiction. Names, characters, places, and incidents either are the products of the author's imagination or are used fictitiously. Any resemblance to actual persons, living or dead, businesses, companies, events, or locales is entirely coincidental.

Published by Redglare Press
Cover by Dark Mojo Designs
Print Formatting by The Madd Formatter

https://bethdolgner.com

CHAPTER ONE

I grasped the cracked wooden handle of the pot and raised it above my head triumphantly. "I found you!" I whisper-shouted.

Behind me, a childlike voice said with a giggle, "Does this mean you're staying a while, then?"

I turned around to see Clara, one of my co-workers at Nightmare Sanctuary Haunted House and a bona fide fairy, standing there with a grin. She was wearing dark sunglasses and a knit cap that was pulled down low over her ears. The sunglasses made sense because it was a sunny day, but the cap looked wildly out of place. It was late summer in Arizona, and everyone else at the yard sale was dressed appropriately for the heat.

Of course, her violet eyes and pointed ears would have looked even more out of place than the knit cap, so I totally understood the disguise.

"Hey!" I said happily. "I see I'm not the only one looking for a deal today. How are you not sweating to death?" I eyed the knit cap.

Clara crossed her arms. "I asked you a question first. If you're buying pots and pans, then does that mean you're staying in Nightmare for a while?"

I looked down at the pot in my hand. It was worn and a bit discolored, but it was still in decent shape. It was, at any rate, the best option out of an entire cardboard box full of old kitchen items. I was hoping I'd have more luck at the next yard sale. "I've been eating out or making a sandwich for every meal," I said. "If I have pots and pans, I'll finally be able to cook for myself."

"You still haven't answered the question."

I smiled self-consciously. "I know. I guess the answer is yes, I'm going to stay for a while. And even if I do make it to San Diego, eventually, I'll leave behind a stocked kitchen in my apartment."

My apartment. The little studio wasn't really mine. It belonged to Cowboy's Corral Motor Lodge, and I was only staying there through the courtesy—and maybe a little bit of sympathy—of one of the owners. I had agreed to do some marketing work for the motel in exchange for the free place to crash.

Clara gave me a look of happy satisfaction. "I'm glad to hear you're not going anywhere. And I'm sure Damien will be happy to know you're sticking around, too." The sarcastic tone on that last part was impossible to miss.

"Yeah, he'll probably throw a party to celebrate." I laughed. Damien Shackleford was a jerk. Yes, he was a jerk who had helped keep me safe when my life had been threatened, but he was still a pretentious man with a great big chip on his shoulder. I knew Clara didn't like Damien any more than I did. None of us at Nightmare Sanctuary had been happy when Damien had strutted in one day to take over his missing father's haunted house attraction.

Clara and I chatted for a few minutes, then we both got down to the business of going through boxes and piles of items to find something worth taking home. In addition to the pot, I also got a small yellow porcelain planter with a succulent in it. I figured it would look pretty on my windowsill. I also found a book of crossword puzzles that had never been written in, thinking I would give it to

Mama as a gift. Since she spent all day, every day at the front desk of Cowboy's Corral, I figured she could use something to help pass the time between welcoming guests.

After I had paid for my finds, I wished Clara good luck and headed to my car. I had gotten it back from Done Right Auto Repair just a week before. Nick Dalton had not only fixed the oil leak that had left me stranded in Nightmare to begin with, but he had put on better brake pads, topped up all the fluids, and gotten the air-conditioner to blast even colder air than before.

I should have gotten a little gift for Nick, too, I thought. I told myself there would be other yard sales and other chances to find a little something to say thank you.

The house that was having the yard sale was on the southern edge of Nightmare. Not that it was very far from anywhere in the little town. It seemed like a long distance from Cowboy's Corral, which was on the northern side of town, but I was back at the motel in a matter of minutes.

Cowboy's Corral had two wings running back from the street, with parking in between. The two-story cinder block office sat up front, between the two lanes leading into and out of the parking lot. I parked in front of my studio apartment, which was on the second floor at the back of the motel, then headed to the front office with the crossword book. When I walked into the office, a man was standing at the Formica countertop. Mama was handing him a key, but she was eyeing him with clear discomfort at the same time.

I hung back and waited for the new guest to continue checking in. The man was asking about good restaurants in town, where to find some nice hiking trails, and that sort of thing. From his side, the conversation seemed completely normal.

Mama, on the other hand, was giving him stiff, short answers. I noticed that after she handed him the key, she took a step back, as if she wanted to put distance between herself and the man.

In just a minute, the man thanked Mama, gave her a little wave, and turned to leave. His round face and brown eyes seemed friendly enough. His sandy hair was a bit unkempt—maybe he should have asked for directions to the nearest barber—but nothing about his looks or his behavior explained why Mama seemed so put off by him.

"What's going on?" I asked as soon as the front door had closed behind the man. "Are you okay?"

Mama didn't answer. Her blue eyes were fixed on the man as he walked past the big front windows.

"Yoo-hoo, Mama Dalton, you there?" I asked. This was getting a little creepy.

Mama blinked rapidly a few times and finally looked at me. "Oh, hey, Olivia. I'm fine."

I leaned my elbows on the counter. "No, you're not."

Mama gave a little shrug, then absently ran her fingers through her fluffy gray waves. "That man, he doesn't feel right to me. I don't think he was being honest with me about who he is or why he's here."

It wasn't the first time Mama had talked about getting vibes from a person, and I wasn't about to argue with her. If she didn't trust this guy, then neither did I. "You want me to keep an eye on him?" I asked.

Mama nodded. "He's in a room downstairs from your apartment. You let me know the second he does anything strange, but don't go putting yourself in a sticky situation."

Wow, so Mama thinks this guy might not just be dishonest, but dangerous, too. I promised her I'd be vigilant, then gave her the crossword puzzle. She thanked me three times before I headed back to my apartment to find the right spot for my new succulent.

I didn't see anything of my suspicious new neighbor before it was time to head to work for the evening. I made the short drive to Nightmare Sanctuary and parked in the grassy field to the left of the four-story stone building. The overgrown front garden and dirt-blackened facade really set the right spooky tone for a haunted house. I was sure the building had been just as imposing a century ago, back when it had been Nightmare Sanctuary Hospital and Asylum, but it had probably looked a lot cleaner and well maintained, at least.

I had just stepped under the portico at the front of the building, heading for the recessed double doors, when I heard someone call my name. I looked over at the window to my right and saw Zach Roth standing there, his long rust-red hair tucked behind his ears and his Nightmare Sanctuary T-shirt tight over his muscular torso. "I hear you made a guy scream last night. Well done!" he said.

"He was so scared he ran out of the room!" I giggled. I had been posted in the hospital vignette inside the haunt the night before, and I had jumped up from behind a silver gurney at just the right moment. Only a few seconds before he started screaming, I had overheard the guy tell his date that Nightmare Sanctuary wasn't actually scary. I had glee-fully proven him wrong.

I gave Zach a wave and continued on inside the building. Zach had a reputation for being in a foul mood nearly all the time—only perking up during the three days of the full moon each month, when he was in his werewolf form —but he had been nice to me ever since I had helped clear his name in a murder investigation. I had gotten to see Zach at work as a werewolf just a week before, and it had been strange and exciting all at the same time. The guests going through the haunted house had just assumed he was a normal person in a costume.

A really, really good costume.

The dining room was about half full when I slid onto a bench at one of the tables. My friend Mori was already there.

She was wearing a plum-colored silk gown that set off her dark skin and burnt-orange eyes beautifully. She smiled, her vampire fangs showing, and said, "Clara says you've been shopping for kitchen things. I'm glad to hear you're staying."

I felt something on my leg, and I looked down to see Mori's pet chupacabra, Felipe, rubbing his gray leathery face against my shin.

"He's glad, too," Mori added.

It was the second time that day someone had expressed pleasure that I wasn't leaving Nightmare. Not leaving yet, at least. I felt my cheeks flush. "Thanks," I said quietly.

I was spared from having to say anything else, since the Sanctuary's acting manager, Justine, stepped up to the podium on a small platform at the far end of the room just then. She had been running things ever since Baxter, the Sanctuary's owner, had disappeared more than six months before. She was still running the day-to-day operations, at least when Damien didn't get in the way. "Good evening, everyone," Justine called. "First, expect a few more guests than we usually have on a Thursday night. The booster club for the Nightmare High School football team has been selling those tickets we donated. Second…"

As Justine continued, I looked around the room, wondering where Theo was. He was the other vampire at the Sanctuary, and he and I had quickly become friends.

"Looking for me?" someone whispered into my ear.

I jumped and slapped a hand over my mouth so I wouldn't let out a startled yell. Theo had snuck up on my right side while I had been looking to my left. "Theo!" I hissed. I didn't want to disrupt the nightly staff meeting—which I liked to think of as a family meeting—so I tried to convey my exasperation with my facial expressions. It only made Theo cover his own mouth to keep from laughing. He was really proud of how well he could sneak up on me.

When Justine announced I would be working in the lagoon vignette that night, Theo gave me a little nudge. "Yay," he said quietly.

I was mostly splitting my time between taking tickets at the front door and working in the lagoon vignette. Last night's spectacular performance in the hospital vignette had been my first time working that particular part of the haunted house.

Once the meeting wrapped up, I made my way to the wardrobe room and got dressed in my usual red coat with lacy cuffs, matching skirt, and tall brown leather boots. I stuffed my shoulder-length auburn hair under a black tri-corner hat. Wearing a pirate costume was becoming second nature, even though I had only been doing it for about three weeks.

The lagoon vignette was an impressive sight. There was a small but detailed replica of a pirate ship in the space, and the walkway guests followed went up onto a catwalk that spanned a shallow pool. Above, faux vines dangled from branches.

But the most impressive part of the vignette was the mermaid inside the large crate that sat in front of the ship. One side of the crate was glass, giving guests a view of Seraphina swimming inside. She was actually a siren, rather than a mermaid, and she was gorgeous despite having a faint green tint to her skin. When I arrived at my post, she was upside down in the crate, her silver tail lifting out of the water. I heard Theo spluttering and knew she had splashed him.

"It's what you get for sneaking up on me again!" I called to him, laughing.

Theo grimaced. "And I can't just dry my face, or I'll rub off all my zombie makeup!"

I was still laughing when the overhead lights flashed

three times, then went out completely. Nightmare Sanctuary Haunted House was open for business.

Late in the night, I had just finished hurrying a group of guests out of our vignette and into the next when I heard a shout. It was Seraphina. She had hoisted herself up so that her entire torso emerged from the top of the crate. She braced herself on the edge and glared down at a man standing just in front of her. "I said stop!" she yelled.

There were a few dull thuds, then she screamed, "I will drown you if you don't stop it right now!"

CHAPTER TWO

Through the dimness, I saw Theo approach the man Seraphina was screaming at. He bent at the waist and deftly hoisted the man over his shoulder. The man yelled in protest while Theo hauled him out like he weighed no more than a child.

As Theo disappeared through a hidden door that led into the network of pathways between the vignettes, I ran over to Seraphina. She was staring in the direction of the door, strands of her wet blonde hair sticking to her face, which was twisted in anger.

Out of the corner of my eye, I could see there were several guests who had witnessed the whole scene, and they were gaping at Seraphina. I caught the eye of one of the other pirates and jerked my head toward the guests. Luckily, he got the hint and immediately began urging them toward the next vignette.

"Are you okay?" I asked Seraphina. I had to crane my neck up to see her, and a few drops of water splashed down from her shoulders.

"I'm fine. That man—"

The rest of Seraphina's sentence was cut off by a loud, high-pitched wail, and I immediately pressed my hands over my ears. Clearly, the banshee had already heard that something had happened to her girlfriend.

Seraphina raised one arm and made a calming gesture. Fiona's wails didn't cease, but they did decrease in volume, and I was able to lower my hands. I turned and saw Fiona running up to Seraphina's crate, her long white gown and her black hair both streaming out behind her. "Sera, what happened?" Her voice, usually deep and smooth, was nearly as high-pitched as her wailing. "I was on my way back from my break, and Theo charged past with a guy over his shoulder. He was shouting about you."

"I'm okay, Fiona," Seraphina said. Despite her repeated assurances, I could see the way her arms shook. "Some man started banging on the glass, and when I surfaced so I could yell at him, he pulled a fishhook out of his pocket."

Fiona let out a sharp, angry wail.

"What's the significance of a fishhook?" I asked.

Seraphina glanced down and gave her tail a swish. Since I was standing right in front of the crate's window, I jumped in surprise at the sudden movement. "It's a threat and an insult," Seraphina said darkly.

Oh, right. Because she's half fish. Even if the man thought Seraphina was just a woman in a mermaid costume, it had still been a mean gesture. I gave a curt nod, feeling silly for not having figured that out myself.

I turned to see if any new guests had entered the vignette and saw that not only had five guests just walked into the room, but so had Clara. She rushed up to Fiona and hissed, "We have guests! We can discuss this after we close for the night!"

Fiona looked at Seraphina grimly, then turned and began walking to the hidden door. Clara followed through it, and the rest of us gave our attention to the guests, who were looking at us with confusion.

One of the other pirates stalked up to the group. He pointed toward the hidden door. "Anyone who doesn't follow the captain's orders gets thrown in the brig! You wouldn't want that, would you?"

Five heads shook, and someone in the group let out a sound that was part laugh, part scream.

"Then get moving!" the pirate shouted. The group obeyed, and I filed in behind them, standing just a little too close to the last person in the group for her own comfort. When she turned and saw me glaring at her menacingly, she jumped and pushed the man in front of her, telling him to move faster.

Ordinarily, I would have gotten a kick out of frightening someone successfully. Instead, I immediately glanced at Seraphina again. She had returned to her spot under the water. Theo came back at some point, but we were too busy with guests for any of us to discuss what had happened.

The last couple hours of the evening dragged by as I replayed the incident over and over in my mind. I hadn't been able to get a good look at the man who had harassed Seraphina, but I immediately thought of the guest who had checked in at Cowboy's Corral that afternoon. Mama had felt like something was off with him, so I couldn't help but wonder if he had been the one causing problems tonight.

Seraphina remained submerged until the Sanctuary closed for the evening. No sooner had the overhead lights come back on following the last guests' exit than Fiona was in the lagoon vignette again. Seraphina finally kicked her tail and broke the surface of the water as we gathered around the crate.

"Did you know the guy?" I asked.

Seraphina shook her head. "No."

"He's never going to get inside the Sanctuary again, that's for sure," Theo said. I wasn't surprised he had joined us without me noticing. Since he was a vampire—albeit one who had somehow lost his fangs—I just assumed his supernatural status gave him incredible stealth.

"Did you get his name?" Fiona asked. I was relieved to hear her voice had returned to its usual husky tone.

Theo shook his head. "No, but we'll find him on the feed from the security cameras and hang his picture inside the ticket window. And when you're in town, Olivia, be on the lookout for a man in his twenties with long, wavy black hair and a tattoo of a skull on the back of his right hand."

"Noted," I said. Of the four of us standing there, I was the only one who ventured into Nightmare on a regular basis. Theo, Fiona, and Seraphina all stuck close to the Sanctuary, where they lived and worked. I also noted the description did not match my new downstairs neighbor at the motel.

Nightmare Sanctuary closed at midnight. Typically, I would be back in my apartment and in bed by a little after one o'clock. Instead, I was still at the Sanctuary at that hour. Word had spread about Seraphina's encounter, and a lot of us wound up huddled in the dining room, discussing it. Finally, when I had yawned twice in the span of a minute, I said good night and headed home.

I didn't get out of bed until nearly lunchtime on Friday. Even though I had been picking up kitchen utensils and cookware over the past week or so, I still got showered, dressed, and made the walk to The Lusty Lunch Counter for a cheeseburger and fries. I had eaten lunch there every day when I first arrived in Nightmare, and I didn't want to stop going completely. I was quickly becoming friends with my usual server, Ella, and I liked the food, so I told myself that going a couple times a week was just fine. Also, between having my car paid for and trading marketing work for my apartment, I didn't even have to worry about money anymore. Not as much, at least.

Despite the summer heat, I found that I preferred

walking to The Lusty rather than driving there. It was only about a fifteen-minute walk, and if I cut down High Noon Boulevard, I could walk under the shade of the covered boardwalks on either side of the street. I had to dodge all the tourists by taking that route, but I could also catch a few minutes of a staged Wild West shootout in the dirt-covered street, which was fun.

The Lusty Lunch Counter was on the street behind High Noon Boulevard, which meant it was a place for locals instead of tourists. The clapboard building had a high facade, and the sun-bleached wood and slightly lopsided balcony made it look more like something from a ghost town rather than the popular, bustling little tourist town that was Nightmare.

Inside, though, the Western look gave way to classic diner. I made a beeline for my usual stool at the stainless steel counter, and soon, Ella was putting a diet soda down in front of me. I could afford to drink something other than water these days, which was a small but significant victory for me.

"Hi, Ella," I said brightly.

"Hello, Olivia," Ella answered in a distracted voice. She was twirling the ends of her chestnut-brown ponytail with her fingers, and her eyes were directed toward the swinging double doors that led into the kitchen.

Someone farther down the counter called Ella's name, and she jumped. "Coming," she called in a shaky voice.

Ella had stopped putting a menu down in front of me more than a week before, when she realized I always got the lunch special of a cheeseburger and fries. In fact, she had started putting my order in the moment I sat down. I was surprised, then, when I slurped down the last of my soda and still didn't have any food in front of me. Ella had been bustling back and forth, busy with the lunch crowd, and finally, I called her name.

"Oh, Olivia, hi." Ella looked faintly surprised. Then, with a self-conscious laugh, she said, "Right. You were already here, and I already said hi. Um, let me refill your drink. I'll put your order in, too."

Before I could ask what was going on, Ella turned and walked away. When she came back with a fresh soda for me, I reached out and lightly touched her arm as she put the glass down. "You okay?" I asked. I realized with a start it was the third time I had asked that question, or some version of it, in just twenty-four hours. First it was Mama, then Seraphina, and now Ella.

Ella hesitated, her brown eyes darting toward the kitchen doors. She bit her lip, then leaned in close to me and said quietly, "There's a new dishwasher who just started here yesterday. I don't know why, but I don't trust him. He gives me the creeps."

My thoughts instantly turned to my new neighbor. He hadn't been the bad guy in Seraphina's story, but maybe he was the villain in Ella's story, instead. If the new dishwasher had started the same day my neighbor had arrived in Nightmare, then it was possible they were one and the same person.

Ella bustled off, and a short time later, I had my lunch in front of me. I was eyeing the kitchen doors as much as Ella, wanting a peek at whoever was behind them.

When I was done eating, I let my gaze rove around the diner. When my eyes reached the booth in the far back corner, I froze.

My new neighbor was sitting there, staring intently in my direction.

I hastily turned around, just as Ella was putting my check down in front of me. She glanced at me and blurted, "What?"

"The man in the back booth is giving *me* the creeps," I

said. Maybe Mama had been right about him. Was he watching me?

Ella quickly glanced that way, then said, "Maybe we can introduce him to our dishwasher, and they can go hang out anywhere that's not here."

"Good idea."

One of the kitchen doors opened, and Ella gasped quietly. "It's him," she whispered.

The new dishwasher had a baseball cap pulled low over his eyes, and his white T-shirt was loose on his thin body. He walked right over to Ella, standing far too close to her, in my opinion. I couldn't hear what he was saying to her, but I could see how intense his gaze was. Ella took a step back, toward me, so she was pressed up against the edge of the counter.

"Wynn," Ella said in a warning tone, her back arching in an attempt to put more space between her face and his.

"Ella," he answered flatly.

I had my mouth open to tell him to watch himself when he reached up and gave one of Ella's giant hoop earrings a gentle tug. Wynn had a tattoo of a skull on the back of his hand.

CHAPTER THREE

The new dishwasher at The Lusty Lunch Counter was the same man who had gotten himself hauled out of the Sanctuary the night before. I sucked in my breath and leaned forward over the counter. "Excuse me," I said firmly.

Wynn turned to me with a fiery glance, and it was even easier to understand why Ella was unnerved. Not only was Wynn crossing a line in his behavior toward her, but he also looked dangerous, almost wild.

"You need to take a step back," I said.

No sooner had I said that than a man's voice called, "Wynn!" I looked up and saw a tall, slightly overweight man who looked to be in his fifties standing with one of the kitchen doors propped open. He ran a hand over his balding head, then gestured for Wynn to return to the kitchen.

Wynn looked at Ella. "See you soon," he said. After a moment, he disappeared into the kitchen again.

Ella let out a shaky breath. When I started to speak, she interrupted me with, "Yeah, I'm all right. He was just making small talk, but…"

I crossed my arms. "But he was making small talk in your personal space. That is not okay. Who can you talk to about him? Who's your manager?"

Ella waved an arm toward the kitchen. "Jeff hired him,

and he owns the diner, so I don't think talking to him about it would do much good."

"I can stick around for a while if you want backup," I said.

"Thanks, but my boyfriend is on his way over. Kyle is about twice the size of Wynn, so I'll be safe." Ella managed to give me a small smile.

I didn't leave until I had encouraged Ella, again, to talk to Jeff about Wynn's behavior. I didn't want to tell her about Seraphina, figuring that would only leave her feeling even more anxious about Wynn, but it was clear the guy had a pattern of acting inappropriately toward women. If the owner of The Lusty had hired a creep, then he needed to know it.

I went home feeling unsettled, too. My neighbor had vacated his spot in the back booth by the time I left, but between his staring and Wynn's behavior, my trip to The Lusty had not been the enjoyable experience I had expected.

At least, I told myself, *I have work tonight to look forward to.*

That was the thought I kept in my mind all afternoon as I sat at the small Formica table in front of the kitchenette in my apartment and prepared social media posts for the motel. I'd had to sell my sleek, modern laptop shortly after the divorce since I had been broke, so Mama had loaned me an ancient, hulking model whose battery didn't even hold a charge anymore. At least it was better than nothing.

I was still looking forward to my night when I arrived in the dining room of the Sanctuary for the family meeting. It was a Friday, which meant big crowds, and more people always made the time go swiftly. Instead of Justine stepping up to the podium to address us, though, it was Damien.

Great. It was never good news when Damien got up to talk.

Damien was wearing a pair of charcoal-gray trousers and a black button-down shirt. He reached up and patted his wavy, light-brown hair before he started to speak, as if he didn't already know it looked perfect. "Good evening," he said.

"Is it?" I heard Mori say under her breath.

"I wanted to address the incident that happened last night in the lagoon vignette," Damien continued. He turned his green eyes toward the table I was sitting at, but I could tell I wasn't the one he was focused on. It was Theo. "We have a reputation to protect. Not just in this community, but with the tourists who come here to enjoy Nightmare Sanctuary. If a guest is breaking any of the rules, or behaving in a way that seems inappropriate for the family atmosphere of this place, then our operational procedures state that you should find a staff member with a radio and ask them to call security."

My jaw dropped. Was Damien really implying Theo hadn't done the right thing by hauling Wynn away from Seraphina? I mean, sure, Theo probably could have done it without throwing the guy over his shoulder, but Wynn had deserved to be ejected. How much more would Wynn have upset Seraphina if Theo had taken the time to find someone with a radio, then waited for security—in other words, Zach—to show up? Besides, Zach probably would have carried Wynn out the same way.

I knew I wasn't the only one who disagreed with Damien's pronouncement. I could hear angry grumbling all around me, and even though she was on the opposite side of the room, I heard Fiona emit a soft wail.

Damien turned things over to Justine shortly after, and as she began to assign roles and update us on a few things, I watched as Damien stalked out of the dining room. I assumed he was going back to his office. He seemed to spend most of his time there, rather than with any of us. He had claimed he showed up to rescue the Sanctuary from its dire financial situation, but word was that the situation wasn't really all that bad. There couldn't possibly be so much paperwork to deal with that Damien had to spend that many hours locked in his office.

It was just a way to avoid dealing with any of us. Damien didn't hide his dislike for the Sanctuary, and he had told me that he was there simply because it was his father's legacy. And, after his father had gone missing about six months before, Damien had finally reached a point where he couldn't ignore the responsibility he felt in Baxter's absence.

I was stationed at my original post that night, which was tearing tickets at the front entrance. The time flew by as I greeted guests, answered the usual questions, and had fun watching people who were already scared and jumping at shadows.

About an hour before closing, Clara sidled up to me. "A few of us are going to Under the Undertaker's after work. Want to join?"

I immediately agreed, and it was only after Clara walked away that I realized the trip to the bar would probably be one long complaint session about Damien. I had once promised Mama to go easy on him, and I tried— usually—to bite my tongue, but that didn't mean I couldn't listen in on the conversation.

Once the Sanctuary closed for the night, I made my way to the locker room to get my purse. Just as I exited, I ran into Gunnar. And I mean I quite literally ran into him. Gargoyles take up a lot of space. Gunnar was tall and broad, and his bat-like wings could only tuck in against his back so much.

"I'm just about to head to Under the Undertaker's,"

Gunnar said after I had walked face-first into his chest. Like the rest of his body, it looked like it was carved from stone and covered in a light layer of green moss. "Want to walk with me?"

I had planned to drive over, but it was a nice night out, and I enjoyed Gunnar's company. I agreed, and before long, Gunnar and I were heading in the direction of High Noon Boulevard. We followed the dirt road that led to the crossroads at the gallows, where I turned left to take my usual route. Instead, Gunnar instructed me to go straight. "This is a bit of a longer walk, but these streets are empty at this time of night," he explained.

Gunnar had to be careful about venturing beyond the Sanctuary since he was a little—make that a lot—conspicuous. The bar we were heading to was a secret place for supernatural creatures, so those who couldn't pass as human could go have a little fun without any risk.

The road we were on was dark, and I kept glancing up to appreciate all the stars that were visible. In Nashville, the bright city lights had outshined most of the stars. Here in Nightmare, they were on full display.

While I was looking up, Gunnar was looking ahead, and he suddenly boomed, "Fiona! Hey, Fi!"

A long way ahead, we could see Fiona gliding along the street. She was impossible to miss, even in the near dark, in her white gown. But instead of responding to Gunnar's call, Fiona continued walking, eventually turning and disappearing from view.

"Does she normally take late-night walks?" I asked.

"She usually sticks to the old cemetery," Gunnar noted.

As we neared High Noon Boulevard, Gunnar's pace slowed, and he moved so that he was walking close to the buildings we passed. I knew he was trying to hide in the shadows, and I acted as a scout of sorts, moving ahead to check if the coast was clear. We made our way like that into the alley that ran behind the buildings along one side of High Noon Boulevard.

Under the Undertaker's was set up like a speakeasy, so the entrance was the back door of a coffee shop, which was housed in what had been the mortuary during Nightmare's early years. Gunnar knocked, and a small window in the door opened. Rose-colored eyes peered out at us. I had only been to the bar once before, but the fairy manning the door seemed to remember me, and she opened it right up for us with a smile and a friendly hello.

We wound down a spiral staircase into the basement, where long curtains were hung to create cozy alcoves for the low tables and stools. The entire bar was lit by candles, giving the whole place a soft, dancing glow.

Theo and Mori were already there, and no sooner had we sat down with them than Justine and Clara came in. A few others from the Sanctuary joined us, too, and I was surprised not to see Fiona. Since she had been moving in the direction of Nightmare's Wild West street, I had expected her to join us.

As I had anticipated, the gathering wound up being a Damien-bashing session. I stayed fairly quiet, though I nodded my head in solidarity a lot as I sipped my beer. Eventually, the topic shifted to happier subjects, but after two hours, I was ready for bed.

Gunnar must have sensed I was tired because he started saying his goodbyes and telling everyone that "we" would see them tomorrow. I said good night, as well, and we were soon flitting from shadow to shadow to get Gunnar safely out of the tourist district.

Once we were back on the lonely road that led in the direction of the Sanctuary, Gunnar and I made small talk. As we chatted, we passed the same low hills that we had on our trip to the bar. This time, though, I heard a man's voice coming from one of the hills.

I stopped and stared in that direction, grabbing Gunnar's arm at the same time. "Did you hear that?" I whispered.

"Hear what?" Gunnar was peering in the same direction as me.

"I heard someone talking. Someone's over there."

The smart thing to do would have been to keep walking back to the Sanctuary, but instead, I made a beeline for where I had heard the phantom voice. As I got closer, I could see there was a wide metal door set in the hillside. It was rusted but solid looking, and it had two padlocks on it: a modern one and another that was probably an antique.

"It's a mine," Gunnar said. "Nightmare had one big copper mine that brought in most of the money, but there were a lot of smaller mines around here, too."

"Well, someone is in there."

Gunnar pointed at the locks. "That would be impossible, unless someone locked them in there."

I frowned. I knew I hadn't been hearing things.

I pressed my ear against the cold metal of the door.

Again, I heard a man's voice. It was faint and had an echo, like it was coming from far inside the mine, but this time, at least, I could understand the words.

"My ashes are my own," the voice said.

CHAPTER FOUR

I let out a cry of surprise and jumped back. Even though I had been listening with the hope of hearing the voice again, I hadn't really expected to. I stumbled on a loose rock, and Gunnar wrapped a strong arm around my waist to hold me steady.

"You heard it that time, right?" I asked breathlessly as I steadied myself.

Gunnar shook his head. "No. Did you hear the voice again?"

"I did. Maybe there's another entrance to this mine? One that's unlocked?"

Gunnar started laughing. "Olivia, I know you love digging for answers, but not tonight, I beg you. Traipsing around these hills in the dark might get you intimate with a cactus. Besides, what if the voice belongs to a regular human? We don't want them seeing me."

"You make some good points," I conceded.

Gunnar shrugged. "You're probably right about there being another entrance, and I expect it's just teenagers sneaking in there to have some fun. There's not much else to do in this town on a Friday night."

I glanced at my watch. "Saturday morning, technically."

It was much later than my usual bedtime when I finally

got back to my apartment. I didn't even bother washing my face before I fell into bed, and I didn't wake up until just before noon on Saturday.

Despite the fact it was lunchtime, I still needed to start my day with a cup of coffee. I had picked up a coffee maker at a yard sale the week before, and even though it looked a little worse for wear, it still made a good pot of coffee. It sure beat drinking the bitter, burned stuff Mama kept in the lobby.

Speaking of Mama, I wanted to give her a rundown of the marketing work I had done the day before, so I took a quick shower, got dressed, and poured another cup of coffee to take with me up to the office. I opened my front door only to find Mama standing there, her hand poised to knock.

"Hey, I was just coming to see——" I stopped short when I saw the shocked look on Mama's face. "What?"

"Have you heard? There's been another murder!"

I'm not going to lie. My first thought was, *Well, thank goodness I wasn't the one to find the body this time!* That was quickly followed by a flood of questions, and I decided to start with, "Who?"

"Jeff over at The Lusty Lunch Counter hired a new dishwasher just this week," Mama said. "They found him this morning, drowned in a sink full of dirty dishes!"

Wynn. I gasped, and I immediately thought of the way he had acted toward both Seraphina and Ella. The guy might be new in town, but he hadn't wasted any time making enemies.

Mama's eyes were wide, and I gently pushed down on her arm, which was still poised to knock on my door. "Come in," I said gently. "You didn't know him, did you?"

"No. I understand he arrived in town just this week." Mama walked inside and plopped down on my loveseat. "Obviously, he's not the only one who's new to Nightmare." Mama raised her eyebrows significantly. "My new guest, Cowan Rhodes… All I'm saying is that it's strange timing."

I nodded. "Someone you got a bad vibe from arrives in town, and the next day, there's a murder. I can see how that would seem suspicious. But," I pointed out, "don't forget that people felt the same way about me. I got to Nightmare just a few days before I found Jared Barker's body, so some of the locals naturally assumed I killed him. And, as we all know, I turned out not to be a murderer."

Mama tried to laugh at that, but it came out as more of a nervous squeak. "I never suspected you, anyway."

I promised Mama I would find out what I could. She looked ready to march down to The Lusty herself, but since her husband was still in Phoenix, taking care of a sick uncle, she was too busy with Cowboy's Corral to go anywhere. Instead, I slurped down the rest of my coffee and walked to the scene of the crime.

The street in front of The Lusty Lunch Counter was filled with what had to be every single police car in Nightmare. Plenty of folks—tourists and locals alike, from the looks of it—were gathered on the far side of the street, watching the spectacle.

Except there really wasn't much to see. I spotted a few officers chatting with folks, but that was about it. I also saw Ella sitting on a bench near the front door. Her knees were pulled up, and she was resting her head on them, so I couldn't see her face.

There was no yellow crime scene tape around the diner, so I marched right up to Ella and sat down. As I put my arm around her shoulders, Ella looked up at me with a tear-stained face. "I was the first person here this morning," she said in a strained voice. "I woke up before dawn, and I couldn't get back to sleep, so I thought I would come to work early and talk to Jeff, like you suggested. But he wasn't here yet, so I let myself in with my key. I went into the kitchen, and… and Wynn was there, bent over the sink. I thought at first it was some kind of joke, but…"

Ella started to cry, and I hugged her close. She might not have liked Wynn in the slightest, but finding a dead body had to have been a shock.

"The police are treating this as a murder, aren't they?" I asked. "But couldn't Wynn have simply drowned? Maybe he passed out and fell forward into the sink."

Ella made a noise that might have been a laugh. "Sure, and he just so happened to fall right onto a dirty knife that was pointed straight at his heart."

That was a little detail Mama had failed to mention. In fact, word about that probably hadn't gotten out yet.

There was another detail I was curious about. "Would Wynn have been the last person to leave the diner before it closed for the night?"

Ella shook her head. "No. In fact, he and I work the same shift. We both got off work at four o'clock yesterday, long before closing time. He must have come back here later for some reason."

Ella looked around, then leaned toward me and said in a low tone, "I'm upset, but I'm also kind of relieved."

"Because of his behavior toward you?" I could understand that some part of Ella was glad she wouldn't have Wynn's eyes boring into her anymore.

"It wasn't just here at work, either. Thursday night, I went to the saloon with a few friends. I don't live too far from there, so I walked over. We had a great night, until I spotted Wynn sitting at the bar. He was turned around on his stool, just staring at me in that creepy way. It was so bad I left early."

"I'm sorry he ruined your evening," I said.

"Oh, it got worse!" Ella's voice rose, and when a police officer nearby glanced over, she cleared her throat, then continued in a quiet voice. "He followed me from the saloon. I was walking along the boardwalk on High Noon Boulevard when I realized he was a little way behind me. There were other people out, too, but it was almost like I could feel him back there, you know?" Ella shivered and wrapped her arms more tightly around her knees.

When Ella didn't continue, I whispered urgently, "What happened next?"

"One of my friends had also left the saloon, and right as I reached the corner, she was driving past. I flagged her down and caught a ride. I have no idea what would have happened if she hadn't rescued me. I was actually planning to come here. Since The Lusty is open late, I figured I could have a cup of coffee and call my boyfriend to come pick me up."

"Smart," I said. "I'm sorry you were in that situation, but, like you said, you don't have to worry about him being a creepy stalker ever again."

The same police officer who had looked at Ella when she rose her voice sauntered up to us. "Miss Griffin? We have some more questions for you. Would you come with me, please?"

I gave Ella's shoulders one last squeeze, then released her with a quiet, "Good luck!" She nodded at me grimly and rose.

As I watched Ella and the officer walking away, my eyes landed on Jeff, the owner of The Lusty. He was running both hands through his thinning hair, strands sticking up in every direction. Either he had been in bed when he got word of the murder at his diner, or he had been making the same nervous motion so much that it had made his hair look like a tumbleweed.

I thought about offering Jeff my condolences, but since I didn't actually know him, I decided against it. Besides, as I watched, a tall, wiry man in a pair of khaki pants and a blue polo shirt approached him. The two seemed to know each other, and after a brief exchange, Jeff shrugged and nodded his head slowly. The other man pulled a small digital tape recorder out of his pants pocket and held it up between the two of them. A reporter.

Curiosity got the best of me, and after I stood, I purposely walked close to Jeff and the reporter. The first words I heard were from Jeff, who said, "I just hired Wynn this week."

The reporter sounded almost gleeful as he asked his next question. "Did you know when you hired him that there's an outstanding warrant for his arrest?"

CHAPTER FIVE

I was so stunned by the reporter's question that I stopped walking. I didn't care if he and Jeff caught me eavesdropping. I wanted to know more about Wynn and this alleged warrant.

Jeff ran his hands through his hair yet again. *Good thing it's not a TV interview,* I thought. He started shaking his head. "No. No, I didn't know. An arrest warrant? For what? He was a good kid. Wynn had just arrived in Nightmare, and he was looking for some work. I just wanted to help the kid out."

There was something about the way Jeff spoke that caught my attention. I didn't think he was lying about not knowing anything about the warrant. If anything, I would have said Jeff sounded more disappointed than shocked by the news.

If Mama were here, she could tell me what kind of vibes Jeff is giving off.

There was a shout from somewhere to my left, and I glanced up in time to see a good-looking man in his early twenties running toward the diner. He had a broad chest and biceps that bulged under his white T-shirt. "Ella!" he shouted.

Ella's boyfriend. He had to be. As I watched, he ran right up to Ella and caught her in a fierce bear hug. The police officer who was questioning Ella stood with his arms crossed and an impatient look on his face, but he didn't interrupt.

I returned my attention to the interview, but the reporter had moved on from talking about the warrant for Wynn's arrest. He was asking Jeff if the police had called him about the murder or driven to his house to deliver the news personally. It didn't seem all that important to me, so I stopped listening and started walking.

There were plenty of questions running through my head. Unfortunately, the one that was most prominent at the moment was whether or not Ella's boyfriend had been involved in Wynn's murder. Surely, I told myself, Ella had relayed the stories of Wynn's disturbing behavior to him, and it was possible he had decided to take matters into his own hands, quite literally. Maybe he had only gone to The Lusty to confront Wynn, and things got out of hand.

I threw a glance at Ella's boyfriend. With his size, he could have easily overpowered Wynn.

Hopefully, before long, the police would have answers about what time Wynn might have died, and why he had returned to the diner so long after his shift had ended. If he had gone there while the diner was still open, any number of people could have slipped inside and killed him. If, on the other hand, Wynn had gone there after closing, then only someone with a key could have gotten inside, unless there were signs of a break-in.

Ella had a key. So did Jeff, of course. Maybe what I had sensed in him during the interview wasn't disappointment but guilt?

Wynn had been brand new in Nightmare, and already, I had a running list of people who might have murdered him. My neighbor Cowan was still at the top of that list. Maybe he had followed Wynn to the diner.

Then my thoughts flitted to Fiona. She had been so

upset over Wynn's behavior toward Seraphina, and just the night before—the same night Wynn was killed—Gunnar and I had seen Fiona walking in the direction of the diner. She had completely ignored Gunnar when he called out to her. Since Seraphina was a siren, drowning Wynn might have seemed like a fitting punishment.

"Oh, no, Liv, don't go there," I mumbled to myself. I didn't want to even consider the idea Fiona might have killed Wynn. Yes, she was a banshee, an Irish mythological creature whose wails were believed to tell of a coming death, but surely, she wasn't the one actually causing the deaths.

I really, really didn't want Fiona to be the guilty party. I made a mental note to ask her where, exactly, she had gone on Friday night. Hopefully, she would have a good answer and maybe even a good alibi.

My plan had been to go straight home, but I suddenly thought of Emmett Kline. His real estate office was close to the diner, and even though he had probably been at home when the murder happened, I thought maybe he had spied Wynn a time or two. I knew he frequented The Lusty, and just maybe, he had seen something of Wynn on his way to or from work.

Emmett's office was in an adobe building just one block down from the diner. The front windows were plastered with printouts of homes, buildings, and land for sale. When I walked inside, Emmett was sitting at his big desk, which took up most of the back wall of the office.

Despite the summer heat, Emmett was, as usual, dressed in a three-piece suit. On this day, he had chosen a navy-blue suit, which set off his white slicked-back hair.

When Emmett looked up and realized who was walking through his door, he actually looked a little frightened for a moment. I couldn't really blame him. The last time we had seen each other, we had both been on the receiving end of a threatening note from a murderer.

"Let me guess, Olivia," Emmett began. "You're somehow involved in the murder at The Lusty, aren't you?"

I laughed self-consciously. "No, but I did come here to ask if you'd seen anything suspicious. Your office is so close to the diner, and I thought maybe you'd seen Wynn around."

"The dead dishwasher? Yeah, I saw him there during lunch on Wednesday. He was talking to Ella about totally normal subjects, but it somehow came off as threatening."

"I saw something similar. Did you see anybody else at the diner acting strangely?" I was thinking of Cowan, my new and suspicious neighbor.

Emmett shook his head. "No." Suddenly, he smirked at me. "If you're not involved with the murder, then why are you asking questions? What's in it for you?"

I sighed and sat down in one of the two chairs in front of Emmett's desk. "Mama—you know, Motor Lodge Mama over at Cowboy's Corral—wanted to know what was going on. I told her I'd walk over to the diner to learn what I could. But then... Well, I just feel like there are some people in this town who aren't being honest." I frowned. I had almost let it slip that I was suspicious of a friend of mine, but I had caught myself at the last minute. The "normal" people of Nightmare tended to think of those who worked at the Sanctuary as weird and untrustworthy under the best of circumstances, and I didn't want to say anything that might upset the tenuous relationship between those two worlds.

Emmett laughed. "Well, if you're going to insist on playing detective, then I will tell you this: I heard Wynn and a friend were sleeping in a van out at Copper Creek Campground. Maybe you can ask his friend for a comprehensive list of Wynn's enemies."

"I'd like to think I'm a little more subtle than that," I said playfully.

"By the way," Emmett said, "I haven't seen you since you helped catch Luke Dawes. Thank you. When you have some free time, I'd like to treat you to dinner."

I started to protest that it wasn't necessary, but Emmett held up a hand to silence me. "I owe you one. I would have been able to buy Barker Ranch even if Jared's killer had ridden off into the sunset, but I know there would have been plenty of gossip that maybe I had been involved in his murder. You know, the villainous real estate agent who will stop at nothing to get his hands on the property he covets."

I blushed and glanced down. For a while, that was exactly who I had thought Emmett was. I was pretty sure he knew it, too.

Anxious to change the subject, I asked, "Are you making any progress in finding Damien a place to live?"

Emmett raised his eyebrows. "Isn't he your boss? I'm surprised you haven't just asked him."

Yeah, sure. Because Damien and I totally had that kind of relationship. Also, I did not like hearing him referred to as my boss. He was, I guess, but only because his father was missing. I preferred to think of Damien as our evil overlord with no mercy, but maybe that was a little extreme. Instead of expressing any of that, I simply said, "He's in his office a lot, so we don't see him much."

"I don't tend to talk about my clients," Emmett said before waggling his eyebrows conspiratorially. "Especially the picky ones!"

I grinned. That sounded about right for Damien. I thanked Emmett for his time and told him I would leave him to it. On my way out of his office, I glanced down the street in the direction of The Lusty Lunch Counter. There were only two police cars out front by that time, and there were definitely fewer people milling about to witness the spectacle.

My mind was still sorting through everything that had happened in the past couple of days as I walked slowly back to the motel. I was hot and hungry, and I resisted the urge to stop in at one of the restaurants on High Noon Boulevard. I hadn't been to any of them, since I had been warned their prices were jacked up because that was where all the tourists were. Instead, I promised myself a home-cooked meal in my apartment.

First, though, I wanted to pay Mama a visit so I could fill her in on everything I had seen and heard at the diner. I also wanted to conspire with her to learn more about Cowan Rhodes. When I walked in the office, though, I heard Mama before I saw her. She was sitting at her desk behind the counter, so all but her hair was hidden from view, but I could hear her crying softly. I ran to the counter and leaned over it as far as I could. "Mama?"

Mama looked up at me, black mascara running down her face. "Oh, Olivia, it just keeps getting worse, doesn't it? Did you see it happen?"

"See what?"

"They arrested that sweet girl Ella! The diner's security camera caught her going into the diner early Saturday morning, about the time they think that guy was killed."

CHAPTER SIX

"Ella told me she went to work early this morning to have a chat with Jeff, the owner, so of course she's on the security footage," I clarified. "I don't know why the police think that makes her the killer. She found Wynn at the sink. She's not a suspect, but the one who alerted the police to the murder."

Mama bit her lip, sniffed loudly, then said, "My friend Nancy Briggs just called me, and she said they handcuffed Ella and put her in the back of a police car. And she overheard Officer Reyes say the video of Ella going into the diner is from three o'clock this morning. That's a little early to show up for a chat with the boss."

I curled my fingers around the edge of the counter in an effort to hold myself up. My knees were suddenly feeling like jelly. Why in the world would Ella have gone to the diner in the middle of the night? For that matter, why would Wynn have been there, especially when the diner would have closed an hour before? Had Ella lied to me about going to work early? "That doesn't make sense," I said quietly. "And they're sure it's Ella on the security camera?"

"Sure enough that they arrested her. Poor girl. She doesn't seem like the murderous type. Maybe that dishwasher attacked her, and she was just defending herself."

"Maybe." My heart broke for Ella. I couldn't imagine someone as sweet as her sitting in a jail cell. I thought about her boyfriend again. This time, though, instead of wondering if he was a suspect, I was fervently hoping he could give her an alibi. Maybe Kyle and Ella had been together Friday night, and he could vouch that she hadn't been at the diner.

I leaned forward and rested my forehead against the counter. The Formica felt cool against my skin, and it helped soothe me a little bit.

"Olivia," Mama said, her voice cracking.

"Yes?"

"I just can't believe that little girl killed someone."

"Me, neither."

"We have to help her."

"I know." I raised my head and looked at Mama. "The best way to help her is to start with the suspect closest to us."

Mama wiped at her round cheeks. "Let me go fix my makeup, and then I'll get online and start digging up what I can on Cowan Rhodes."

"And I'll keep a close eye on him. Ella's going to come out of this just fine." I wasn't sure if I was reassuring myself or Mama.

When I arrived at the Sanctuary shortly before seven o'clock that evening, there were already a few people in line at the ticket window. The haunted house wouldn't even open for more than an hour. I trudged into the dining room, feeling like the day's events were a physical weight on my shoulders.

Mori knew something was off the second I slid onto one of the benches. "Spill it," she said. I could tell she was trying to use her hypnotic gaze on me, because I got a strange sensation, almost like a tugging at my mind. It was exactly what Mori used to lure tourists into secluded areas so she could drink some of their blood, then send them off with no memory of the event.

I brought both hands up in front of my face in a warding-off gesture. "Okay, but you don't have to use your super vampire powers to get me to talk." I lowered my hands, all sense of levity gone, and filled her in on the murder and Ella's arrest. I ended with, "I just don't think Ella killed him. We spoke today, before she was arrested. She was in shock, of course, but she wasn't acting like someone who had just committed murder."

"How old is this girl?" Mori asked.

"Early twenties, I would guess."

Mori narrowed her eyes. "Is she incredibly strong? Or is the man who died very small?"

I caught Mori's drift. "You're wondering if Ella would have been able to hold Wynn down long enough to drown him. Or to stab him through the heart. I'm honestly not sure which came first, but I guess an autopsy will figure that out."

A man spoke from my left-hand side. Theo had joined us, silently settling onto the bench next to me. "Somebody really wanted that guy dead if they killed him twice."

"Yeah. And to answer your question, Mori, Ella is shorter and smaller than Wynn. For someone of her size to physically overpower him, he would have to have been drugged or drunk or something."

"Then let's hope the autopsy shows the victim didn't have anything unusual in his system," Theo said. He gave me a reassuring smile. He hadn't put on his zombie makeup yet, so instead of looking scary and threatening, the smile just highlighted how handsome he was. "If we're discussing this girl's size, then I'm sure the police are, too. They'll probably come to the same conclusion that she couldn't have killed him."

I blew out a breath. "You're right, Theo. We have to

trust that Ella won't be sitting in jail for long. I have to admit, though, I would love to get my hands on that video footage. I'm still having a hard time believing Ella just wandered into the diner at three in the morning."

"So let's get a peek at it," Mori said.

"It's not like I can waltz into the police station and ask to see it," I responded.

"Of course you can." Mori grinned. "Well, I can."

I blinked at Mori a few times, wondering what she meant. Her gaze was making me feel a little sleepy. "Oh! You can mesmerize them and convince them to show it to you!"

"Exactly."

I was just opening my mouth to respond when Justine called all of us to attention. The family meeting seemed to drag on forever. I didn't realize I was impatiently bouncing one leg until I felt two paws wrap around my calf. I glanced down to see Felipe swatting at me. Apparently, he thought we were playing a game of "catch the leg." I forced myself to sit still, and he eventually gave up and crawled into Mori's lap.

As soon as Justine ended the meeting, Theo leaned forward. "Don't forget, Mori, Olivia is part of Nightmare's normal world, too. We don't want to do anything that might get her in trouble with the police."

Mori set her lips in a thin line. "True."

"So we don't go to the police," I suggested. "They got the security footage from Jeff, the owner of the diner. He probably still has a copy. Why don't we ask him?"

"I'm more comfortable with that idea," Theo agreed.

"It is a better plan," Mori conceded. "I can't control people with my mesmerizing. I can only influence them, and it doesn't work on those who are strong mentally. I tried it on you a couple of times, Olivia, when we first met."

"I know. I could feel it."

"Because you're strong. You felt it and rejected my influence. One man will be a lot easier to mesmerize than an entire police station. Let's go to the diner after work tonight."

Theo and I agreed, and then it was time for all of us to get ready for work. I headed up to my post at the front door, where I would be tearing tickets. As much as I enjoyed working in one of the vignettes, I had to admit I also liked not having to put on a costume and do my makeup. Zach was already selling tickets, so I just gave him a wave when he glanced in my direction.

I was grateful it was a Saturday, the Sanctuary's busiest night of the week, because if the crowds had been thin, I would have spent most of my time looking at my watch and tapping my foot. Instead, I had a constant stream of people coming through the door, and the time passed quickly.

Mori and I usually had a break around the same time, and when we passed each other in the dining room, she told me to simply meet at the front entrance after the Sanctuary closed for the night, and we'd head to The Lusty. I volunteered to drive. I was pretty sure neither Mori nor Theo owned a car.

Once the last guests of the night had exited the building, I hurried to the locker room to retrieve my purse, then returned to the front doors. Mori joined me after a few minutes, and I stared at her, open mouthed. Her hair was still piled on top of her head in a high coiffure, but the rest of her look was all modern. She was wearing skinny jeans, a low-cut gold silk blouse, and high heels with a leopard print on them. I was wearing jeans and my Nightmare Sanctuary T-shirt, and I felt frumpy compared to her. "Wow," I finally said. "But you do know we're going to a diner, and not a club, right?"

Mori tugged her blouse just a little lower and gave me a wicked smile. "Whatever helps us get a look at the video, right? Besides, I plan to make an appearance at Under the Undertaker's after we're done. I want to make an entrance."

When Theo joined us, I saw he had also dressed for going out into the "normal" world. He had on black jeans and a gray T-shirt. Still, I started laughing as he got closer. He hadn't quite removed all of his makeup. "You look like you're wearing a ton of black eyeliner," I said.

Theo raised an eyebrow. "I think I look good."

He was right. The makeup made his brown eyes stand out, and I agreed that he was rocking the look.

"All right," I said. "We're all here. Let's go."

"No, we've got one more coming," Theo said.

I immediately thought of Damien, but I brightened when Malcolm appeared in the doorway. "I'm ready," he said, tipping his top hat toward me. Unlike Mori and Theo, Malcolm had not bothered to change. He was still wearing a black suit and a long black cape, which only emphasized how tall and skinny he was.

I briefly considered suggesting Malcom take off the cape, then stopped myself. Why should I care what the guy wanted to wear out? We were going to be an odd-looking group at The Lusty no matter what.

It was nearly one o'clock in the morning when we walked into The Lusty Lunch Counter, so I was surprised to see just how many people were there. In fact, there was only one free booth, which we crowded into while half the place stared at us and whispered to their neighbors. I could tell by the judgmental looks that they weren't all captivated by Mori, who looked downright sexy. Instead, they were gaping at Malcolm. Even if he had changed into some-thing less old-fashioned looking, he still would have stood out like a sore thumb. A very skinny sore thumb with sunken cheeks and pale skin.

I wasn't even sure what kind of supernatural creature Malcolm was. I'd seen him outside in broad daylight, so he wasn't a vampire.

The server who came over to our table looked slightly uncomfortable. We quickly ordered a round of coffee, and she walked away with a relieved expression. As soon as she was gone, Mori grabbed my hand. "Let's go," she said.

Mori led me through the diner and up to the cash register at one end of the counter. "Is Jeff here? I wanted to say hi," Mori said smoothly to the server standing there. His face went slack, and he started to reach toward Mori, a twenty-dollar bill in his hand. "No, honey, I don't want your money. I just want to see Jeff."

The man nodded and motioned us to walk behind the counter. "He's in his office," he said in a breathy voice.

As we walked the length of the counter toward the double doors leading to the kitchen, Mori looked back at me and snickered. "I wasn't even trying that hard with him! He would have offered up his car if I'd been giving it my all."

I shuddered when we entered the kitchen and I saw the big stainless steel sink, which had police tape still wrapped around it. Someone was washing plates in a smaller sink nearby.

The office was a tiny space, no bigger than a closet, at the far side of the kitchen. Jeff was sitting in there at a desk, looking exhausted and stressed. Mori moved into the open doorway and knocked lightly against the frame. "Hi, there," she said. "We just wanted to thank you for a great dinner. We're so sorry about the tragedy that happened here. Is it true one of your servers killed a dishwasher?"

Jeff nodded slowly, already entranced. His eyes had a glazed look, and his mouth hung open.

Mori leaned down and put a hand on Jeff's shoulder. "Can we please have a peek at the security camera footage from last night?"

Jeff nodded again, then turned to his computer. In a few clicks, a black-and-white video popped up on the screen.

The video showed the counter, the serving area behind it, and the kitchen doors. The timestamp in the upper right-hand corner had Saturday's date and the time: *3:17 a.m.*

Someone appeared at the bottom of the screen, walking slowly behind the counter toward the kitchen. The video showed the person from the back, but the high pony-tail and big hoop earrings were visible.

Halfway to the kitchen, the person paused and turned toward the counter, making their profile perfectly clear.

It was definitely Ella.

CHAPTER SEVEN

I pressed my lips together and clamped my hands tightly over them. I didn't want to make a peep, afraid that if I did, it might break the hypnotic spell Mori had put on Jeff. He played the video clip three more times for us, and every time, I felt more horrified. Ella really had been inside The Lusty in the middle of the night. I still couldn't fathom why.

My eyes were fixed on the computer screen as Mori began talking to Jeff in a coaxing voice again. I was too focused on that profile shot of Ella to listen to what Mori was saying, but suddenly, the video footage disappeared, replaced by an email program. Jeff started typing away, and I realized Mori was giving him an email address.

"Thank you ever so much," Mori said a moment later. I felt one of her hands pushing gently against me, and I took it as a cue to back away from the door to Jeff's office. Mori followed me, keeping her eyes on Jeff until we were halfway across the kitchen. Then, she turned and hustled us out of there.

It wasn't until we were sitting in the booth again that I spoke, and then, it was only a quiet thank you. Mori had gotten me exactly what I wanted—a look at the security video that allegedly proved Ella had killed Wynn—even though I was regretting the request. I had thought it would be blurry, or inconclusive, or something that would convince me it wasn't Ella in the video but someone else.

But there was no mistaking that it had, in fact, been Ella.

The server had brought our coffees while Mori and I had been in the kitchen, but I just stared down into the steaming black liquid. Malcolm reached over and put a bony hand over mine. "Come on," he said quietly. I looked up and saw Theo putting cash down in the middle of the table.

We got up and left. If people were still staring at us, I didn't notice.

I started walking in the direction of my car, but Theo put a gentle arm around my shoulders. "We're heading to Under the Undertaker's," he said. "We want to talk about this in a place where we won't be under a microscope."

Before long, the four of us were seated around a low table in the basement bar, and Mori put her cell phone down in the middle of the table so we could all see the screen. "I got him to email it to me," she explained as Theo and Malcolm peered at the security footage that started playing. I almost laughed at the idea of a vampire having email and a cell phone.

"I don't know the girl, but I assume that's your friend?" Malcolm asked me.

I nodded. "But look at the way she's moving," I said. I hadn't really noticed on the first three viewings—I had been in too much shock when I realized it really was Ella in the video—but she was moving stiffly, like her joints weren't bending properly. "Ella is graceful, smooth. She can carry a tray full of drinks without spilling a drop. Why would she suddenly move in such a jerky fashion?"

"Earlier, you suggested the dishwasher might have been drunk or drugged," Mori said hesitantly. "Perhaps your friend was drunk. It could explain why she might have done something so out of character for her."

"Actually," Malcolm said, leaning closer to the screen, "the way she's moving makes me think of a zombie."

"Oh, have you met a lot of zombies?" I asked sarcastically.

"A few."

Before I could ask Malcolm to elaborate, Theo said, "She looks like she's sleepwalking. I think that's more likely than the idea Ella was hit with temporary zombie disease."

I looked sharply at Theo. "Is that a real thing?"

"No. Sorry, Olivia, I shouldn't be joking when the situation looks so dire for your friend."

"It's okay. After this day, I probably need a joke or two."

"We definitely need drinks," Mori said, even as she turned around and waved down a server, giving them a big smile. I wondered if she ever used her mesmerizing ability to get better service in restaurants, then remembered Mori didn't go to restaurants since she didn't need to eat food.

It was three o'clock—around the same time Wynn had been, apparently, murdered by Ella—by the time I got home and into bed. I still didn't believe Ella really had murdered Wynn, and I felt more determined than ever to track down the truth.

When I woke up on Sunday, though, I realized that before I could set out to clear Ella's name, I needed to go grocery shopping. Now that I had those pots and pans, it was time to use them.

I had found the local grocery store shortly after I had decided I was going to stay in Nightmare for a while and couldn't afford to eat out for every meal. On the few occasions I had been there, I had noticed how often I saw shoppers greeting each other and having conversations in the aisles. I wasn't used to living in such a small town, where so many people knew each other.

But I was new in town, which meant I was unlikely to have a "How are your kids?" kind of conversation in the middle of the produce section. I was surprised, then, when I was pushing my cart down the bread aisle and felt a tap on my shoulder as I heard a man say, "Oh, hello."

I turned and saw a man with a small smile and bright hazel eyes. I didn't recognize him until I glanced down and saw his green polo shirt and khaki pants. It was the journalist who had been talking to Jeff outside the diner.

"Hi." I said it as more of a question than a statement.

"I saw you yesterday, at The Lusty." The man stuck out a hand. "I'm Ross Banning from *The Nightmare Journal*."

"Olivia Kendrick," I said, shaking his hand. "Nice to meet you."

"I saw you talking to Ella Griffin shortly before she was arrested. Are you two friends? Do you know her well?"

"Oh, well, actually…"

"We can do this right here, real quick, if that's okay," Ross said. He reached into a pocket and pulled out his digital tape recorder. "I've only got a few minutes to spare. I've got to get over to the campground to talk to the victim's traveling companion. If I were that guy, I'd get out of town as soon as possible, so I want to catch him before he hits the road."

"What do you mean?" I asked, eyeing the tape recorder. If Ross thought he was going to do an interview with me about Ella, then he was gravely mistaken. "Do you think someone is going to go after Wynn's friend, too?"

Before Ross could answer, I saw movement out of the corner of my eye. I looked over to see Damien, who was wearing the mirrored sunglasses he so often sported. Seriously? We were in the middle of a grocery store. Did he actually think he looked cool? He was also the nicest-dressed guy in the place, which made him stick out even more.

Damien stepped close to Ross. "Leave her in peace," he said. There was a note of warning in his tone.

"Olivia and I were just getting to know each other," Ross said smoothly. I noticed he had already slid the tape recorder back into his pocket.

"You were going to coerce her into talking about the murder. She's trying to do her shopping. Leave her alone."

Ross's friendly expression turned dark. "You're the kid of that missing man who owns Nightmare Sanctuary, aren't you? I've seen you around. I look forward to the opportunity to interview you about how things are going there."

Damien stiffened, but he didn't back down. "Leave Olivia alone."

Ross moved slightly toward Damien, a sneer on his face. I expected him to start yelling, and I shrank back. I didn't want to get caught up in a brawl in the middle of the bread aisle. Ross seemed to think better of it, though, because he snorted out a breath and said, "I guess I'll have to find another time to interview Ms. Kendrick. I have every right to ask her what she knows about the suspect."

"And she has every right to refuse to speak to you," Damien countered.

I wanted to tell Damien he was absolutely right, yet there he was, making the decision for me. I was also annoyed he had interrupted my conversation with Ross. I still wanted to know why the reporter thought Wynn's companion might want to hightail it out of Nightmare. If Ross believed the guy might be the next target, then it indicated he didn't really think Ella was guilty, either, and that Wynn's actual murderer was still at large. Ross's remarks also meant Wynn's friend must feel the same way.

Before I could articulate any of that, or even repeat my

question to Ross, he turned on his heel and stormed off. I could practically feel the anger stretching between him and Damien as the distance between them grew.

I was still staring toward the end of the aisle after Ross had turned and disappeared, presumably heading for the exit, when Damien said in a gruff tone, "You okay?"

I whipped my head toward him. "No, I'm not okay," I said, a little more forcefully than I had intended. "I've had to ask Mama, Seraphina, and Ella that same question this weekend, and Ella has been accused of murder, and it's entirely possible the guy staying in the motel room below my apartment is the actual killer. I am not okay, Damien."

Damien's eyebrows rose above the top edge of his sunglasses. Apparently, he was as surprised by my outburst as I was. "Granting Ross an interview would have only made things worse for you. He wasn't here when I left Nightmare twenty years ago. I hear he's written some really unflattering stories about the Sanctuary, though."

"Then I'm surprised you two aren't buddies, since you say a lot of unflattering things about the Sanctuary, too."

Damien glared at me. I couldn't see his eyes, but I could still tell he was giving me a look that could kill under those mirrored shades. After a moment, he said quietly, "It's different."

I rolled my eyes heavenward. If Damien thought being the owner's son gave him the right to trash-talk the haunted house, then I was going to have to teach him better manners. Yelling at him wasn't going to do it. Instead, I put on my best polite smile and said, "Thank you for rescuing me from the big, scary reporter. If you'll excuse me, I have food to buy." I turned to my right and started pushing my cart along the aisle.

Damien kept pace with me, walking silently at my side, until I stopped and said, "I don't need an escort."

"Ross might try to ambush you while you're putting your groceries in your trunk. I'm staying with you."

"Fine. In that case, can you please grab me a jar of crunchy peanut butter? It's behind you on the middle shelf."

Damien complied, and once he had tossed the jar in my cart, I added, "Ross won't be waiting for me. He said he has to get to the campground to interview Wynn's buddy before the guy heads for the hills. Ross seemed to think he was in danger."

"That's a strange assumption when the police think they've already caught the killer."

"Agreed." I looked at my list. "Oops, we walked right past the coffee. Can you get a bag of light roast? Ground, not whole bean, please."

I had to admit, I was kind of enjoying making Damien do my shopping for me. It would teach him not to butt in to my life. I wasn't quite sure why he felt the need to defend me in the first place, when he didn't even seem to like me.

I only had a few more things on my list, and soon, we were waiting in line to check out. "At least the murder doesn't involve the Sanctuary this time," I said, "though I do hate that Ella is involved. Wynn had been harassing her at work, and he followed her out of the saloon one night. I even saw him acting like a creepy stalker right there in the middle of the diner."

Damien took off his sunglasses—finally—and peered at me. Quietly, almost too low for me to hear, he said, "Are you sure you didn't wish him right out of her life?"

CHAPTER EIGHT

When I was a kid, my mother used to tell me not to roll my eyes so much, or they would get stuck pointing up, and I would trip over things when I walked. If there was any truth to that, then this visit to the grocery store might be the thing that made my eyeballs permanently look up.

"Oh, come on!" I said loudly. The person checking out in front of us turned and looked at me curiously, and even the woman at the cash register spared me a glance while she scanned a cereal box. When I spoke again, I kept my voice almost as low as Damien's. "Are you really implying that me and my mysterious conjuror skills are responsible for Wynn's death?"

"I think it's a possibility we have to consider." There was no trace of humor in Damien's voice.

My mouth was working really hard to form words, but nothing was coming out. Damien had already told me he thought I was some kind of supernaturally talented human called a conjuror. Someone who could wish for something so hard they actually made it happen. He was convinced it was how I had found a job notice for the Sanctuary, even though the position hadn't existed. Somehow, Damien believed, I had willed the job into existence.

Part of me wanted to tell Damien he was being utterly ridiculous, but another part of me was offended. "I would never wish for somebody to die!" I hissed. Okay, maybe I had thought about it a few times during my messy divorce, but I hadn't really *meant* it.

"I'm not saying that's what you did," Damien said. "But I do think your abilities are greater than you realize."

"I don't have any abilities."

"My point exactly. You're not taking this seriously. If you're a conjuror, Olivia, you could be really dangerous. You need to learn to control your abilities, or bad things might happen. Maybe something bad already did happen."

Again, my eyes were in grave danger of becoming stuck in the skyward position. "I'm not responsible for Wynn's death. Besides, what am I supposed to do? Go to magic school to learn how to reel in my awesome power?"

Damien completely ignored the sarcasm. "I'm offering to give you lessons. I can teach you to tamp down your abilities, to keep your magic under control."

Thank goodness it was our turn at the cash register then, because I did not know how to respond to that. This was the most bizarre shopping trip I had ever been on.

True to his word, Damien escorted me all the way to my car. He even helped load my bags into the trunk. "I told you Ross wouldn't stick around," I said. "He's probably got his tape recorder in Wynn's friend's face already."

"If he bothers you again, you let me know." Damien hesitated. "I'll see you tonight."

"Yeah." Was I supposed to thank Damien for his totally unsolicited "help"? Mama's admonition that I should be kind to Damien came back to me, and I said begrudgingly, "Thanks for looking out for me."

Damien nodded briefly in acknowledgement and walked off toward his silver Corvette. His car stuck out in the parking lot as much as Damien had stuck out inside the store. It was only as I watched him pull onto the street with a screech of his tires that I realized he hadn't bought anything.

Once I got back to my apartment, I put away my groceries while pondering the things Damien had said about my alleged supernatural skills. I had to admit there was some tiny part of me that worried I had, in fact, killed Wynn. With my mind. The whole idea of it was laughable, but there was just enough of a *What if?* in my thoughts that I felt uncomfortable.

While I made myself lunch, I muttered a lot of nasty things about Damien for even putting the idea in my head. Mama would never know I was trash-talking him since I was only saying it to myself.

By the time I had eaten, my mind was made up: I was going to go downstairs and meet Cowan Rhodes. No matter what that video footage made it look like, I knew deep down Ella hadn't killed Wynn. I didn't know why she had been at the diner at three in the morning, but I did know she was innocent. If I was going to help her, then it made sense to start with the suspect who was closest to me.

Cowan's room was on the ground floor of the motel. It wasn't directly underneath my apartment, but it was close. I walked to his door, took a deep breath, and knocked.

There was no answer. I knocked again but still nothing.

I had amped myself up for the meeting, and I could feel my nervous energy coursing through me with nowhere to go. Since Cowan wasn't home, I walked up to the front office to see Mama. The walk would at least work off some of the energy.

Mama reported she hadn't been able to track down anything about Cowan online. "There are plenty of people with that name," she said, "but no one who sticks out as being this particular Cowan Rhodes."

"I'm going to talk to him. I tried just now, but he wasn't home."

"Just be careful."

"Who cleans the rooms here? When I was still in a regular motel room, I was always out whenever they came by to tidy up."

Mama seemed to know exactly what I was thinking. "That's my cousin Barb who does the cleaning, and she's not going to be doing any snooping around for us. Besides, when Cowan checked in, he requested no one come in to make up his room. He seems to want privacy."

"So much for that angle," I said. "And I wasn't going to make Barb go rooting through Cowan's things. I was just going to ask her if she had seen anything unusual in his room."

Mama chuckled. "If only it were that easy to catch criminals! My guess is that if Cowan has anything to hide, he's not going to leave it sitting out in the open."

"Solving murders would be a lot easier if the killers were stupid," I noted.

"True. However, even if we did get into Cowan's room, we wouldn't know what to look for. We don't even know if he has anything to do with the dead dishwasher."

"I think he's a more likely suspect than Ella. Unfortunately, it's not looking good for her." I briefly told Mama what I had seen in the video footage. Instead of looking upset, like I had expected, her face actually lit up.

"Security cams! Of course!" Mama sat down at her desk. "This place has cameras, and there's one on each side of this building, trained at the driveways into and out of the parking lot. Let's see if anyone was coming or going around the time of the murder."

I waited impatiently while Mama scrolled through the online archives of the Cowboy's Corral security videos. When she gasped, I leaned as far as I could over the counter, trying to crane my neck in a way that would let me see the screen.

"Come around," Mama instructed, waving her arm. "There's a door built into the side of the counter."

I hurried around the counter and let myself into the area where Mama was sitting. I leaned forward and peered over her shoulder.

"See that old Dodge pickup? That's Cowan's." Mama pointed at the truck, but it really wasn't necessary since it took up most of the screen. It was on its way out of the parking area. The timestamp on the video showed that Cowan had left the motel shortly after midnight on the night Wynn had been killed.

"I'm guessing he wasn't running out for a late-night snack," I said. "When did he come back?"

Mama started fast-forwarding through the video. It wasn't until the time in the corner read *5:00 a.m.* that Cowan's truck could be seen returning.

"He was gone for five hours," I muttered.

"He was gone during the timeframe of the dishwasher's death." Mama turned in her chair and looked up at me. "Olivia, do you think I have a murderer staying at my motel?"

I squeezed Mama's shoulder. "I can't say for sure, but you definitely have someone very suspicious staying at your motel."

I had hoped visiting Mama would run off some of my anxious energy, but it only seemed to have increased it. Even if Cowan hadn't had anything to do with Wynn's murder, the fact he had been gone nearly all night was suspicious in and of itself. There weren't a lot of places in Nightmare that stayed open late, like The Lusty and the saloon, and even those places were closed by two o'clock. Under the Undertaker's was open until practically breakfast time, but I doubted Cowan even knew about its existence, and he certainly wasn't hanging out there.

On my walk from the office to the back corner of the

motel where my apartment was, I realized the very Dodge pickup truck we had been looking at on Mama's computer screen was now parked right in front of me. Cowan had returned sometime while Mama and I had been poring over the security camera footage.

I was even more nervous when I knocked on Cowan's door this time, but I was also more determined than ever. I wanted answers.

"Who is it?" Cowan called sharply.

"Olivia. I live upstairs from you," I answered loudly.

The door opened just a crack, and I could only see part of Cowan's face as he gazed out at me. "What do you want?"

"To introduce myself. I understand you might be staying a while, so I figure if we're going to be neighbors, I should say hello."

"What makes you think I'm staying a while?" The one eye I could see narrowed.

I waved vaguely in the direction of the office. "I'm the one who came into the office when you were checking in. Mama mentioned you might be a long-term guest, like me."

In answer, Cowan's eye just narrowed even more.

"Anyway, if you need any recommendations on where to grab a bite or anything, feel free to come ask. I'm usually around during the day."

Cowan nodded slowly. "Oh, yeah. You work nights, over at the haunted house."

"Exactly." *How does he know?*

"You're right. I might just stick around Nightmare for a while. Do you know any cheap apartments for rent?"

"No, but I do know a local real estate agent. He might know of something."

"How about jobs? I can't rent a place if I don't have any money."

"There's a community job board over at the Chamber of Commerce. I'll be happy to give you directions."

Cowan winked at me. At least, I think he did. Since I couldn't see his other eye, it was entirely possible he was simply blinking in a really strange way. "Are they hiring at the haunted house? I feel like I might fit in there."

CHAPTER NINE

My eyebrows shot up. Cowan had said he might fit in at Nightmare Sanctuary as if he knew its secret. Was my new neighbor supernatural? He was out in the daylight, so he definitely wasn't a vampire. His ears were normal, so he wasn't a fairy. Maybe he was a werewolf, like Zach. Or, maybe, his abilities didn't manifest physically. Justine seemed to be an ordinary human, but she had telekinetic abilities.

I didn't want to assume Cowan knew the Sanctuary was a haven for supernatural creatures, so I just smiled and said, "I'll ask tonight whether there are any open positions."

"I appreciate it, Olivia." With that, Cowan shut the door, leaving me to stand there, stunned.

I couldn't tell Mama what had just happened. She was part of Nightmare's normal world, and I couldn't dash up to the office to tell her that not only was Cowan a possible killer, but he was probably supernatural, too. She would think I was nuts.

I went back to my apartment, where I wound up pacing back and forth across the little living area. At the rate I was going, I would wear a path in the orange shag carpet within the hour. The thought I kept coming back to was that I needed to see Ella. I was sure she had told her story to the police a dozen times already, but I wanted to hear it myself. Plus, I wanted her to know that I supported her.

It had only been three weeks since I had visited the police station. Then, it had been to give a statement about nearly getting killed by a UFO hunter. I was more nervous this time around. I parked on the curb and walked in slowly. The Nightmare police station was a quiet place on a Sunday afternoon. The officer sitting at the desk just inside the front door was reading a newspaper, and he didn't even bother to look up when I walked in.

"Um, excuse me?" I asked timidly. I wasn't sure why I was so nervous. Maybe it was because I had never visited someone who was in jail before.

The officer lowered his paper just enough so he could peer at me over the top of the sports section. "You're the one who helped us put away Luke Dawes."

"Yes. Olivia Kendrick. Hi. I'm actually here to see Ella Griffin…" I trailed off as the officer folded his newspaper loudly, slapped it down on the desk, and laughed.

"If you're hoping to solve another murder, you're too late. We caught her red-handed."

I folded my arms over my chest. "You have a video clip that she appears in briefly, nothing more."

The look of mirth on the officer's face disappeared, and he eyed me sharply. "How do you know about the video?"

Think fast, Liv! I smiled. Or I tried to, at least. "I haven't been in Nightmare long, but I've already been added to the gossip hotline."

The officer stared me down, and I could feel the corners of my mouth twitching as I tried to hold his gaze and keep my smile in place. Eventually, he harrumphed and jerked a thumb over his shoulder. "Fine. Go through both sets of doors. You have ten minutes."

I muttered a hasty thanks as I followed the officer's directions. I had been through the first door before. It led to a long hallway that had offices along it. The door at the end of the hallway was nothing fancy: just a wooden door painted white with a diamond-shaped window in it. I had expected it to be metal, at least.

The door might not have been what I associated with small-town police station jails, but once I was through the door, it was everything I had expected. There were four small jail cells in all, two on each side of a short hallway, complete with steel bars. Only one of them was occupied. Ella was sitting on a cot with her legs crossed and her head in her hands. She didn't even bother to look up when I walked in.

I wasn't sure how I was supposed to start the conversation, so I settled for a quiet *hi*. Ella looked up when she heard my voice, then she jumped up from the cot and came over to stand in front of me. Her hand snaked through the bars and grasped mine. "Olivia! What are you doing here?"

"I came to see you, of course."

"That's so kind of you. You just missed Kyle."

"Your boyfriend?" I asked.

Ella nodded. "He's been so sweet through all of this. He says he knows I didn't kill Wynn."

"I know you didn't kill Wynn, too."

Ella's eyes filled with tears, and her mouth twisted as if she were about to cry. "But the police are convinced I did. They say there's video of me going into The Lusty at three a.m. But I didn't, Olivia. I didn't get there until six, when I went in and found Wynn drowned in the sink."

I narrowed my eyes. "You haven't seen the video?"

"No." Ella paused, then her eyes widened. "You have, though, haven't you?"

I nodded. "Don't tell anyone, because I do not want to explain how I saw it. It's you in the video, Ella, but you're moving weirdly. Someone suggested that you look like you're sleepwalking."

"I didn't kill Wynn in my sleep, if that's what you're thinking," Ella said defensively.

"I believe you. Was your boyfriend with you Friday night? Can he give you an alibi?"

Ella shook her head, her expression a mixture of sadness and confusion. "Kyle came over that night. We ordered pizza and watched a movie, and I fell asleep on the couch. I don't even remember him leaving."

"He just left without telling you?"

Ella laughed weakly. "He says I woke up, kissed him good night, and fell right back to sleep. I don't remember it, though. I was worn out from a busy shift."

"What time did he leave?"

"Kyle says he left around one in the morning."

I sighed. Not only did Ella not have an alibi, but the timing of Kyle's departure didn't look great for him, either. If he had known about Wynn's behavior toward Ella, then maybe he had decided to do something about it. Ella wasn't big and strong enough to overpower Wynn, but Kyle was. When I had seen him outside the diner on Saturday, his biceps had looked about twice the size of Wynn's.

Ella didn't seem to realize her admission looked bad for Kyle. Instead, she was still pondering what I had said about the video. "I don't sleepwalk. What was I wearing in the video, anyway?"

I thought back. "Jeans and The Lusty Lunch Counter T-shirt you always wear at work."

"I changed into pajama shorts and a tank top when I

got home on Friday. Why would I have put on my work uniform to go kill someone, anyway?"

"Because you didn't kill anyone. Maybe someone doctored the video. Maybe it's old footage with a new timestamp. We thought you looked like you were sleep-walking, but maybe you were balancing dishes we couldn't see, or the floor was slippery, something like that."

"Oh, there's definitely a special way to walk when the floor behind the counter is wet. I'm sure there's old footage of me trying to get past a spill." Ella's face got the look like she was about to start crying again. "But who would want to frame me for murder?"

I looked at Ella grimly and squeezed her hand. "A killer who doesn't want to get caught. It's probably nothing personal against you." I thought of Luke Dawes, who had left the body of Jared Barker in front of the Sanctuary, figuring the police would go after someone who worked there for the murder. It hadn't been personal. It had simply been a way to shift the blame. "Anyone who saw Wynn with you would know you didn't like him. Someone is pointing the finger at you because it makes for the perfect story. A young woman defends herself against a creep."

"I don't want to spend the rest of my life in jail," Ella said. She had finally given in and started crying.

"You won't. I promise."

I left the jail, feeling both reassured and rattled. The reassurance came from the fact Ella was still claiming she hadn't set foot in the diner until early Saturday morning, shortly before opening, to talk to Jeff. She seemed to be telling the truth about that. I was rattled because I had to wonder if her boyfriend, Kyle, had killed Wynn, then framed his own girlfriend for the crime.

Or, maybe, Cowan Rhodes had done it, then doctored the security camera video to make it look like Ella was guilty. He had been in the diner the same day I was, so he had observed Wynn and Ella's conversation, too.

All I knew for sure was that we—me, Mama, and anyone else who wanted to join us—had to help clear Ella's name.

When I got to the Sanctuary that night, I ran into Malcolm in the entry hall. He didn't even bother to say hello before asking, "How's your friend doing?"

"She's doing as well as she can, considering," I said. I squeezed Malcolm's thin arm. "Thanks for asking."

"I think many of us here know what it feels like to be falsely accused and ostracized."

Mori had once told me a lot of the supernatural creatures who found their way to the Sanctuary had been outcasts in their hometowns. Some of them had even been forced to leave. When Mori had told me that, I didn't know the secret of the Sanctuary yet, and I had naturally assumed everyone there was human. Just normal, regular humans who didn't quite fit in with the rest of the world. Even now that I knew otherwise, Mori's point was just as relevant: the Sanctuary was a safe haven for those who didn't belong in the regular world.

Malcolm and I walked together to the dining room, and although he didn't usually sit with Mori, Theo, and me, he settled in right next to me on the bench. Mori and Theo arrived a few minutes later, and soon, all four of us had our heads together. I told them about Cowan's comment that he needed a job and thought he would fit right in at the Sanctuary. "There was just something about the way he said it, you know?" I concluded. "Like he knows about us."

I realized the irony of saying "us" since I wasn't supernatural—despite what Damien kept saying—but I still considered myself a part of the team at the Sanctuary. I was in on the secret, and I kept that secret dutifully, and that alone made me one of them.

"Let's find out what this Cowan really is," Mori said. "Maybe Justine can offer him a job interview."

"Or we give him tickets and tell him to come check the place out," Theo suggested. "We can all get a sniff of him as he walks through."

I wrinkled my nose. "Can you really smell the supernatural?"

"Sometimes. The next time you're close to Zach, take a big sniff. There's a definite undertone of dog hair."

I laughed, then quickly returned to the subject at hand. "I don't think it's a good idea for Cowan to come anywhere near this place. Mama doesn't trust him, and I worry that he's dangerous."

"I'll go talk to him," said a voice behind me.

I turned to see Madge, one of the three witches at the Sanctuary. She was the middle one in age, probably somewhere in her twenties, with long blonde hair that always looked like it was caught in a light breeze. She smiled, which made her look even more beautiful. "I have a way with men. I can get him to talk."

We made a plan for Madge to "drop by" to visit me the next day. I was sure that between her looks and her magic, she would be able to wring some answers out of Cowan.

I felt good about having a plan in place, and I was able to stop thinking about both Ella and Wynn while I tore tickets and greeted guests. When I got home and spied Cowan's truck parked outside his room, I smiled to myself. "Tomorrow, we learn your secrets," I said softly.

Madge arrived the next afternoon at two o'clock. We stood by my front door, making small talk while keeping watch for any sign of Cowan. We only had to wait about twenty minutes before he appeared. He walked to his truck, opened the passenger-side door, and began rummaging around. Madge wasted no time in flying down the steps toward him, while I followed at a slower pace.

"Excuse me, sir!" Madge called in a flirtatious voice. "I was just telling my friend that I need a strong man to help me with—" Madge stopped talking as soon as Cowan turned to face her. She gasped and shrank back. "Robert?"

CHAPTER TEN

Madge and Cowan stared at each other silently for so long even I felt awkward, and I was just a bystander. Madge's chest heaved under her sunny orange dress, and she said, "Robert, what are you doing here? And where have you been?"

Cowan waved a hand. "Traveling. And it's Cowan now."

"You changed your name? Why? What are you hiding from? Robert, what's going on?" Madge reached toward Cowan but stopped just short of putting her hand on his arm.

"Nothing is going on. I... I didn't know you were in Nightmare now."

"If you're not here to see me, then why are you in Nightmare?" Madge's initial shock sounded like it was giving way to anger.

I didn't want Madge to get even more upset, so I stepped forward and said, "How do you two know each other?"

Madge kept her eyes fixed on Cowan as she said with a sneer, "We were in love once. At least, I thought we were. Then Robert just disappeared one day, and I never heard from him again."

No wonder Mama had gotten a weird vibe from Cowan when he checked in. I couldn't believe it was just coincidence that he had come to the same small town where his former girlfriend lived. Not only that, but there also had to be a reason he had changed his name. Cowan was definitely hiding something.

"You wouldn't understand, Madge," Cowan said quietly. "I had to leave."

"Why?"

"I told you, you wouldn't understand. I can't talk about it."

When Madge spoke again, her voice was quiet and even. "I loved you."

"I know." Cowan looked away, and I thought I saw something like sadness or regret flit across his face.

"Did you really not come to Nightmare to see me?" Madge glanced toward me. "Olivia said you were interested in getting a job at Nightmare Sanctuary."

Cowan fixed his gaze on Madge again. "Do you work there, too?"

"Of course. It's how Olivia and I know each other. She said you want to work there."

"I might need a job if I'm going to stay a while," Cowan mumbled. "But I don't want to… I wouldn't… It's probably best if you and I don't work at the same place. That might be…"

"Super awkward?" I supplied.

Cowan nodded. He seemed like a different person than the one I had just talked to the day before. Instead of gruff, he was acting almost scared.

Madge turned to me. "Olivia, will you please take me home now?"

"I'll grab my keys." I sprinted up the stairs to my apartment, snatched up my car keys and purse, then dashed back down. Madge was already standing by my car, and

Cowan had disappeared, probably back into his room. I really couldn't blame him.

As soon as Madge and I were in the car, she said, "I'll tell you everything I know about Robert—er, Cowan—when we get back to the Sanctuary, but I don't think he's a killer. He's a terrible person who deserted me, but that's a lot different than committing murder."

I spared a quick glance at Madge as I backed out of my parking space. "I'm sorry he hurt you. And I'm sorry you had to get such a shock today. You were just trying to help Ella, and you wound up getting the emotional version of a slap in the face."

"Honestly, it's kind of nice to know he's still alive. I spent a lot of years wondering what it would be like if I saw him again, and what I would say. Now I know."

Madge stayed silent the rest of the short drive to the Sanctuary. I parked close to the old hospital building, not worried about taking a prime parking spot, since there were no guests in the middle of the afternoon. When we walked through the front doors, I automatically turned right, to head down the hallway that led toward the dining room, but Madge moved toward the grand stone staircase.

I hurried after her. Even though I had been working at the Sanctuary for a few weeks, I hadn't ventured beyond the ground floor. I did know, though, that the old hospital rooms on the upper floors had been converted into rooms for those who chose to live at the Sanctuary.

Madge led me up to the second floor, then turned and headed a short way along the East wing before walking through a door on our right. I followed, expecting to see a small room with a bed and maybe a chair or desk. Instead, I found myself in a cozy sitting room with a couple of overstuffed chairs, an antique loveseat, and thick rugs scattered across the floor.

The other two witches were there. Maida was sitting on

the loveseat. She was wearing her usual black dress and white tights, but her black, pointy-toed boots were sitting on the floor next to her. Her feet swung slowly while she read a book. Morgan's tiny old body looked like it was being swallowed by the chair she was sitting in. Her long black dress was too big for her, making her appear even smaller under her halo of wispy gray hair.

Morgan dropped the knitting that was in her hands as soon as Madge and I walked into the room. "You're upset," she said gravely.

"You met a ghost," Maida added, closing her book and looking up.

"But not a spirit," Morgan said.

"Someone from your past." Maida stood and ran to Madge, then hugged her tightly around the waist.

I still wasn't used to the odd way the three witches spoke to each other, and sometimes to me, but I appreciated their obvious affection for each other. Maida stepped back and took both Madge and me by the hand. "Come, sit and tell us all," she said. Maida looked like she was ten or eleven years old, but she spoke like someone who was much older and wiser.

"I'll put the kettle on." Morgan rose and walked through an open doorway. I spied a kitchen beyond. Apparently, the hospital rooms had been renovated and connected to create small apartments, and I wondered briefly if each witch had their own bedroom, or if they shared one. For some reason, I pictured three twin beds all in a row, with black quilts covering them.

Madge and I settled onto the loveseat, squeezing in on either side of Maida. As soon as Morgan returned from the kitchen, Madge began her story. She explained she had met the man she called Robert when she and the other witches had been living in San Francisco. Madge stopped and looked at me. "We were only there for a couple of years. A coven there needed our help."

"I remember Robert," Maida said. "He was nice until he wasn't there anymore."

Madge nodded. "He and I met at a farmer's market. I was buying fresh herbs for some spell work, and I saw him. We started talking, and he asked me out. We spent every day together for several months. I never told him I was a witch, of course. He made me happy."

"Then, one day, he didn't," Morgan said. She rose at the sound of the kettle whistling and returned to the kitchen.

"Like she said, Robert just wasn't there one day. I called, but he didn't answer. I went to his apartment, and it was empty. There was no warning and no goodbye." Madge wiped at a tear on her cheek. "I really loved him, and I had thought he really loved me. I was heartbroken."

"I'm sorry," I said again, but it was even more heartfelt this time. I knew how much it hurt to love someone and lose them, though Mark certainly hadn't disappeared on me. He had just spent all our money and divorced me. In fact, I realized, maybe Madge had gotten the better deal. At least Cowan hadn't left her high and dry. He had just left her. "You said on the drive here that you don't think Cowan could have killed Wynn, but it sounds like you didn't really know him at all. Not the real him, at any rate."

"My magic helps me see through lies," Madge said.

Morgan shuffled back into the room, carrying a tray laden with four teacups, a sugar bowl, and a delicate milk pitcher. She put the tray down and deftly added two sugar cubes and a dash of milk to one of the cups, then handed it to Madge.

Madge cradled the cup in both hands and blew on the

steaming tea before saying, "Robert was himself in San Francisco. Whoever he is now is the lie."

"You saw him today, and your past became your present," Morgan said as she sat down.

Madge quickly explained her encounter at the motel. "He said he didn't know I was here. I believe he was telling the truth," she concluded.

I wasn't so sure about that. "Why else would he be in Nightmare?" I asked.

"I'll leave it to you to find out." Madge took a sip of tea. "He's not supernatural, by the way. Ro—Cowan—is just a man."

Maybe I had been overreacting to Cowan's comment about fitting in at the Sanctuary. Maybe he hadn't been referring to supernatural creatures, but to people who simply lived on the fringes of the community. At least the question of whether or not Cowan was supernatural had been answered, though our method of finding out had created a lot more questions.

Madge calmed down considerably as we all sipped our tea in silence. Even I felt better, more calm. At least, I felt that way until I got back to the motel. Cowan's truck was still there, and I dreaded running into him. I wasn't sure I would know what to say after the bizarre reunion he'd just had with his ex-girlfriend.

I spent the rest of my afternoon in the front office, sitting in one of the chairs in the lobby while balancing the old laptop on my knees. So far, I hadn't mentioned anything about Cowan and Madge to Mama. I knew Mama thought people who worked at the Sanctuary were weird, and I didn't want to make her even more suspicious of someone whom I considered a friend. I needed to tell her, but I was being a chicken.

I had just finished loading some posts onto the motel's social media accounts when the bell on the front office door tinkled wildly. I looked up to see Lucy, Mama's grand-daughter, rushing through the door. She got halfway across the lobby before she spotted me, and she instantly changed course to head in my direction.

"Miss Olivia! Hey!" Lucy ran right up to me and threw her arms around me.

"Hi, Lucy. How are you?"

As Lucy began chattering away, I saw her dad, Nick Dalton, come through the door. He moved at a slower pace than his daughter. I gave Nick a smile and a wave, then froze when I noticed someone was right behind Nick. It was Cowan.

I quickly averted my gaze, looking again at Lucy. I could just see Cowan out of the corner of my eye as he walked up to the counter and spoke quietly to Mama. Just a couple minutes later, he left. As soon as the door closed behind him, Mama called my name loudly. Lucy instantly fell quiet, and her eyes got round, as if she knew what that tone meant.

"Yes?" I said meekly.

"Do you want to tell me what that was about?"

"What what was about?"

Mama pursed her lips disapprovingly. "You and Cowan Rhodes doing everything possible not to look at each other."

I sighed. It was time to get over myself and tell Mama what had happened. "One of my co-workers came over today," I began haltingly. "And we ran into Cowan down-stairs, when he was getting something out of his truck. It turns out, they know each other. They actually used to date, but back then, Cowan went by the name of Robert."

"Which co-worker?" Mama asked.

I wasn't sure why it mattered, but I answered, "One of the three witch characters at the Sanctuary."

Mama's expression didn't change. If anything, she

looked even more disapproving. She crossed her arms over her chest. "Let me guess: he used to be in love with Madge?"

CHAPTER ELEVEN

I really wished you could call a "time out" in life like you can in games, because I wanted to stand up, form a capital *T* with my hands, and shout, "Time out!"

I did the next best thing. I jumped up—barely grabbing my laptop before it fell out of my lap and onto the floor—and said, "What? You know Madge?"

Lucy started bouncing up and down on the toes of her pink sneakers, her thick, curly dark hair bobbing along with her body. "Ooh, Grandma, you know Maida's mama?" Lucy looked at me. "Or is she Maida's big sister?"

I didn't know the answer to that, and at the moment, I didn't care. Mama seemed to have shrunk slightly, and she picked at a spot on the countertop with a fingernail. "It's a small town, Olivia," she said in a slightly affronted tone. "Just because I don't hang out with the people from the Sanctuary doesn't mean I don't know a few of them."

"Madge said she met Cowan when she and her two companions moved to San Francisco for a few years. Did you know her before then?"

Mama nodded. "She and the other two came to Nightmare at least twenty-five years ago, I'd say. They moved to San Francisco around ten years ago, then came back."

"Twenty-five years ago? No, that can't be right. Madge

would have been a child, maybe even just a baby, and Maida wouldn't have been born yet."

"My math isn't wrong. Madge is older than you think."

I wanted to argue that Maida was only a child about Lucy's age. She couldn't possibly have shown up in Nightmare twenty-five years ago. Either Mama was mistaken, or there was another witch living with Madge and Morgan back then. Whichever answer was correct, it was clear Mama knew quite a bit about the witches.

There was obviously more to the story, but I couldn't ask in front of Nick and Lucy. Nick was looking from his mother to me, his faded blue eyes taking in every word. Nick always looked a little messy—he seemed to be one of those mechanics who was perpetually covered in oil—but he was sharp. As for Lucy, I knew she had no idea the people she had seen when she and I had gone through Nightmare Sanctuary were real witches and vampires and other supernatural creatures, and I certainly wasn't going to break the news to her.

"Anyway," I said, "this raises a lot of questions. Why did Cowan change his name from Robert, did he come to Nightmare looking for Madge—he says he didn't, but I don't think we can take his word for it—and what is he really up to?"

"Who's Cowan?" Lucy asked.

"A guest," Mama said gently. "Olivia and I were just trying to figure out why he's visiting Nightmare. Luckily for us, we get at least another week to decide. He just extended his stay."

Nick looked sharply at Mama. "Do you need me to check up on the guy?"

Mama looked from Nick to me, then back to Nick. "I don't think so. At least, not yet."

"Okay." Nick didn't look as confident as he sounded. "We were just stopping by to say hi, but I'm thinking we might stay for a while. We can order dinner and eat here."

"Yes, please!" Lucy said, clapping her hands. She didn't seem to understand Nick wasn't sticking around just for the fun of it, and I was sure she didn't notice the way Nick kept glancing out the windows, like he expected Cowan to come back.

"Olivia, why don't you join us? The haunted house is closed tonight, right?" Mama asked. She still looked slightly uncomfortable, as if I might call her out at any moment about knowing Madge.

I quickly agreed, then suggested Lucy and I could go pick up food while Nick stayed at the motel. Everyone was amenable to that idea, and before long, we had called in an order at an Italian restaurant just a mile down the road.

Lucy stayed bouncy and energetic right until we were in the car, and I was pulling onto the main road that led into downtown Nightmare. She instantly sobered and said quietly, "Who was that man that came in? The one who knows Maida's mom... sister... um, the pretty witch."

"His name is Cowan," I explained. "He just arrived in Nightmare last week, and his room is below my apartment."

"Oh." Lucy was silent for a few moments. Then, in a voice so low that I barely heard her over the hum of the engine and the air-conditioning, she added, "I didn't like him. He gave me a bad feeling."

I whipped my head so fast to look at Lucy that I nearly swerved out of my lane. "What do you mean?"

"It's hard to explain. It's like..." Lucy tilted her head and stared out the windshield. "Like when my mama washes her hair, and it smells so good afterward. It's like there's all this good-smelling air around her. The man felt like that but the opposite. There was bad air around him. I couldn't smell it, but I could feel it."

"Bad vibes," I mumbled. Lucy had, apparently, inherited her grandmother's gift of sensing things about people. "Lucy, do you get feelings like that about other people, too?"

"Sometimes. You feel good. One day, when I got to school, my teacher felt sad. And I once saw a little girl on the playground who felt really, really bad."

"Was she a mean girl?"

"I don't know. I turned around, and when I looked again, she was gone."

Lucy had said it so innocently, but I felt a chill wash over me. I was almost certain the little girl hadn't been a living one, but Lucy didn't seem to realize she might have encountered a ghost. I didn't want to scare her, so I simply said, "It's a good thing she left, since she felt so bad."

"Yeah, that was lucky." Lucy sat up a little straighter and pointed. "There's the restaurant! Spaghetti Western!"

I turned right into the restaurant parking lot, and by the time we got out of the car, it was like our conversation had never happened. Lucy had gotten her thoughts off her chest, and she had moved on to revving herself up for dinner. I admired her resilience, especially since it was a lot harder for me to brush off what she had said.

Lucy's enthusiasm and the smell wafting from the take-out bags perked me up significantly on the drive back to the motel, and before long we were all diving into heaping platefuls of food. I had ordered lasagna, and I was only halfway through when I declared the rest was going home with me to be tomorrow's dinner. I was stuffed.

I left at the same time as Nick and Lucy. I still wanted to know more about Mama and Madge, but I figured I would wait and ask Madge about it sometime. She would probably be a lot more forthcoming than Mama if there was more to tell than the "it's a small town" excuse.

I tried to go to bed earlier than usual on my two nights

off, but it was getting hard to do. I was surprised how quickly I was acclimating to working from seven until midnight, and not crawling under the covers until one. Or later, if I went out with work friends.

Actually, work friends had been the people I would go out with in Nashville, staying up way too late to either celebrate or commiserate with cocktails, depending on how a marketing event we'd planned had turned out. They hadn't really been friends of any kind, as I had learned. When they found out I was completely broke, and I showed up to work one day in a beat-up used car instead of my sleek sports car, they had started treating me like a pariah. When I no longer had money or social status, I wasn't worth being nice to.

My original plan hadn't been to leave Nashville, or even to quit my job. Quitting was the last thing I wanted to do when I desperately needed every penny of every paycheck. But I had been made to feel like such an outcast that, one day, I just couldn't take it anymore. I gave up looking for a cheap apartment in Nashville—which I was pretty sure didn't exist, anyway—and made plans to go live with my brother and sister-in-law in San Diego. Even going to the opposite side of the country didn't seem like it was far enough away from the people I had thought were my friends.

Here in Nightmare, though, the people I worked with weren't casual work friends. They were something more. Despite everything going on, I went to sleep that night with thoughts of gratitude.

Since I also had Tuesdays off, I had decided it would be another chance to indulge in a Lusty Lunch Counter cheeseburger rather than making something at home. I thought about not going. After all, Ella wouldn't be there, and chatting with her was half the appeal. Still, though, I wanted to support the diner through what had to be a really awful time for everyone who worked there.

It was a good thing I walked instead of driving. There were no parking spots available on the street near The Lusty. Inside, it was just as packed. I should have known the diner didn't really need my support when they were still dishing up fresh gossip. Still, I went on inside and managed to snag a stool someone had just vacated at the counter.

There were a couple of tourists sitting to my right, and after I ordered, I overheard them planning their afternoon, which included catching the staged shootout between Tanner and McCrory. The two cowboys had famously killed each other on High Noon Boulevard more than a century before, and every day, two actors recreated the scene for tourists.

It took longer than usual for my cheeseburger and fries to arrive since the diner was so busy. As my server slid the plate in front of me, I eagerly grabbed the bun with both hands. As I did, the man sitting to my left looked at the server and said, "I hear they got the big sink working again."

"Yeah, the police are finally letting us use it."

My mouth was already open to take a big bite, and I froze. The plate in front of me had been washed in the sink Wynn had been drowned in.

Ew. I'm eating off a murder plate.

I put my cheeseburger down, threw some cash on the counter, and left. I was too grossed out to stick around.

As I began my walk back to the motel, not even feeling hungry despite giving up my lunch, I saw movement in the narrow alley between The Lusty and the building next to it. There were two men standing a short distance down the alley, and I instantly recognized them as Cowan and Jeff.

I hopped backward so they wouldn't see me. The two of them appeared to be deep in conversation, and they seemed to know each other. I risked a peek around the corner of the building, and I could see Jeff gesturing in an agitated manner. Whatever Cowan and Jeff were discussing, it was clearly an intense conversation.

As I watched, Cowan pulled a long knife out of an inner pocket of his denim jacket and brandished it right under Jeff's nose.

CHAPTER TWELVE

I hastily ducked back so I wouldn't be spotted, even though only a fraction of my head had been visible. The last thing I needed was my super-suspicious neighbor knowing I had seen him threatening someone with a knife. I listened hard but didn't hear any screaming, so I assumed Jeff was not in the process of being murdered by Cowan. I must have looked scared and anxious because a couple strolling past looked at me, then veered away from the building to give me a wide berth. I risked a quick glance into the alley again, and I was relieved to see Cowan had put the knife away, and he and Jeff were again talking.

My normal route back to the motel would take me right across the mouth of the alley. Instead, I walked in the opposite direction. I was willing to go a little out of my way to avoid being seen by Cowan. By the time I had made it one block over to High Noon Boulevard, I had decided I didn't really want to head back home. Sitting in my apartment all day would just be boring, and, for the first time, I didn't entirely trust Mama. Hanging out with her in the front office might feel a little strange. That left me with… well, not a lot of options, outside of the tourist attractions.

I was halfway down the street when I made the spontaneous decision to go to the saloon. Mama had told me locals tended to avoid the place on the weekends, since it was full of tourists then. If I were lucky, it would be jam-packed with them, even though it was the middle of a Tuesday afternoon. The idea of being in a big crowd of people who were having a good time seemed comforting. I could blend into the crowd and not have to wonder if anyone around me had played a part in Wynn's murder.

It would have looked a lot cooler to swagger through the short swinging doors that led into the saloon, but instead, I hurried in, then stopped and let my eyes adjust to the dim lighting. Compared to the glare of the afternoon sun, it was downright dark inside Nightmare Saloon.

As my eyes adjusted, I was happy to see the place was pretty packed. The bar had a few open stools, so I made my way to one and hopped up onto it. I felt a sense of calm instantly wash over me. I could just sit and have a drink, like I hadn't just seen a man being threatened with a knife.

Actually, I wasn't as calm as I had thought, because when the bartender asked me what I wanted to drink, I nearly jumped right off my stool. Even though I had the day off, it still felt a little too early to order a beer. I went with an old-fashioned sarsaparilla instead. I wasn't even sure what it would taste like, but I had seen enough Western movies to know that was the thing to order.

As it turned out, sarsaparilla was just a fancy name for root beer. Still, I sipped at my drink while I casually surveyed the saloon. The dark wood paneling and floors really gave the place an authentic look, and I even spotted a few of the servers dressed up like saloon girls. A low stage along one wall had a heavy red curtain with gold trim, and a sign announced an "Old West" vaudeville show on weekend evenings. The saloon was just as touristy as every-thing else along High Noon Boulevard, but for some reason, I liked it. The make-believe Wild West atmosphere felt like an escape from the world.

I was getting to the bottom of my sarsaparilla and considering ordering another when my eyes landed on one of the few people in Nightmare whom I didn't want to see. Ross Banning, the reporter from *The Nightmare Journal*, had just stood up from a table full of tourists in matching T-shirts.

I instantly turned back to the bar, hoping he hadn't spotted me. There was a long mirror on the wall behind the bar, and a quick glance showed me that Ross had definitely seen me. He was already walking in my direction.

"Olivia, we meet again," Ross said jovially as I turned to face him.

"Ross," I said flatly.

Ross glanced around. "I see Damien Shackleford isn't here to protect you." Ross said the word "protect" like Damien's confrontation with him at the grocery store had been a big joke.

"Why would he need to protect me?" I asked in a mock-innocent voice. "I'm sure you're a professional."

Ross hopped up onto the free stool next to me, flagged down the bartender, and ordered a diet soda before he returned his attention to me. He placed his tape recorder on the bar, then raised both hands slightly, as if he were surrendering. "It's not on. I'm not going to interrogate you, as Damien seemed to think. I just want to know what you can tell me about Ella Griffin. Everyone who's ever eaten at The Lusty Lunch Counter knows she's a sweet girl. She's been serving me coffee and pancakes every Friday morning for the past three years. I certainly never thought she seemed like a killer."

"Because she's not."

"And yet, she's sitting in jail right now. I refuse to believe that everyone in this town is surprised by what happened. Somebody out there must have gotten a sense that Ella has a violent streak."

I shook my head decisively. "Nope. She's a sweet girl, like you said."

Ross sighed, and his shoulders slumped. "Do you know how frustrating it is to have a murder case to cover, and nothing to say about it? I can't find a single person willing to go on record about Ella. It's like the whole town is conspiring to protect her."

I waved a hand toward Ross. "That's your story, right there."

When Ross frowned at me, I continued, "Write about how small towns rally to help each other out. Write about the newcomer who showed up in Nightmare, only to get murdered, yet no one seems to be on his side in this. Write about how no one seems to believe Ella actually killed a man."

Ross chewed his lip thoughtfully. "What are you, Ella's PR manager?"

I laughed. "I used to work in marketing. I guess it shows sometimes. I'm always looking for the interesting angle."

"Me, too."

"Speaking of interesting angles," I said, struck with a sudden thought. "You probably know a lot of the prominent people in Nightmare. What can you tell me about Jeff, the owner of The Lusty?"

Ross looked surprised, then he grinned. "I see. You're going to turn the tables on the reporter, is that it?"

"I'm just trying to figure out who all the players are in this murder case. I'm new in town, so any insight you can give me would be really helpful."

Ross seemed flattered that I would ask him to give me the gossip about locals, and after taking a long drink of his soda, he began, "Jeff Crosley isn't a Nightmare native. He came here, oh, seven or eight years ago, maybe. The old brothel was practically falling apart, but Jeff saw potential in it. He bought the building, renovated it, and opened the diner. Where he got all the money for that, no one knows. It seems he had made a lot of money wherever he was before he arrived in Nightmare."

"You don't know where he came from?"

"No. It may have come up in conversation back when I first met him, when I was covering the renovation for the paper, but I can't remember." Ross shrugged. "I wish I could tell you he's some wild character who provides endless fodder for newspaper stories, but he's not. Jeff is just a regular guy. His life mostly revolves around running the diner, though he's also very active with the Nightmare Historical Society. Now that he's worked so hard and spent so much money to get the old brothel looking good again, he wants to make sure some developer doesn't come along and build a four-story modern apartment building right behind it."

"I get that. We had a similar debate in Nashville about how to make room for more people without ruining the historic charm. I guess it's a problem for towns of every size."

"Indeed. If Emmett Kline had his way, we'd have new luxury condos and houses from here to the interstate."

I suppressed a laugh. Emmett's ambitions were well known.

Thinking of Emmett made me think of Jared Barker. With his murder, everyone had seemed suspicious, including his own wife. With Wynn's murder, though, no one seemed to be a likely suspect, with the exception of Cowan. Ella was too sweet, Jeff was just a normal guy trying to run a business, and even though Ella's boyfriend was on my suspect list, he hadn't actually said or done anything—to my knowledge—that made him seem like a top candidate.

"I'm running out of people to talk to," I said to myself.

Ross smiled. "In your quest to prove Ella's innocence?"

When I nodded, he held up a finger. "I'm going to do you a favor, but remember, the day may come when I want you to go on record."

"Go on record about what?"

"Anything. Maybe this murder case, maybe some other juicy story down the road. I help you now, you help me later. Deal?"

I frowned at Ross. I didn't like the idea of being beholden to a reporter. Then again, I didn't have anything to hide. Well, there was the secret of the Sanctuary, but if Ross ever—for some reason I couldn't even imagine—asked me whether the people there were actually supernatural, I would lie through my teeth. "Deal," I said begrudgingly.

"The victim came to Nightmare with a guy who calls himself Claw. They set up at Copper Creek, in the camping and hiking area. Claw is still there, and you can find him in a gray van with Idaho plates."

Even though I had known Wynn was traveling with someone else, I hadn't considered talking to him. This guy Claw wouldn't know the people of Nightmare, so he probably couldn't point me toward a likely suspect.

Unless he *was* a suspect. Ross had a look in his hazel eyes like there was more to the story. When Ross had mentioned Wynn's friend during our encounter at the grocery store, I had thought Claw might be the next victim. I hadn't considered the other possibility. "You think he might have some helpful intel?" I asked.

"I think you should cover all your bases. You gave me some marketing advice earlier, and now I'm giving you some journalism advice. Talk to as many sources as you can." Ross looked back at the tables behind us. The crowd was thinning a little. "Speaking of which, I need to get back to it. I'm working on a story about the drinking habits of Nightmare tourists."

I gave Ross a wave. "Thanks for the tip."

I finished my sarsaparilla, paid, and headed back to the motel. I didn't even go upstairs to the apartment. Instead, I headed straight to my car. It was only after I was pulling onto the main road that I realized I had zero idea where this campground was.

I made a U-turn and parked in front of the motel office. As soon as I told Mama where I needed directions to and why, she pointed at me. "You be careful, Olivia. I don't want you putting yourself in a dangerous situation."

It took a little work to coax directions out of Mama. She wanted me to wait until Damien could go with me, but I firmly rejected that idea. When I promised I was on my way there as soon as we wrapped up our chat, in broad daylight, she sighed and gave in.

Copper Creek Campground and Recreation Area was two miles south of town, but it felt like a different state. The dirt road that led to it wound down into a shallow valley, which was clogged with trees and grassy weeds. It was the greenest place I had seen since I had arrived in Arizona.

The campground was spread out under tall oak trees, and the narrow Copper Creek bustled along one side. Only about a quarter of the camping spots were occupied, so I easily found the gray van from Idaho. There was no answer when I knocked on the sliding door, so I settled onto a nearby bench to wait. It was pleasant under the trees, cooler and more humid than in town.

The sound of the creek cascading over rocks was soothing, and I closed my eyes and inhaled deeply just as a voice said in my ear, "What are you doing here?"

CHAPTER THIRTEEN

The voice was feminine but lower than a typical woman's voice. I knew it was Fiona without even turning around, and her late-night walk toward The Lusty on Friday evening came to mind. I had totally forgotten she was still on my suspect list, too.

Fiona came around the bench and sat down next to me. She had her dark hair pulled back in a braid, and she was wearing a wide black sun hat. Her ankle-length gray dress looked like it might have come from the Victorian era. She had changed out of her usual long white dress, probably so she wouldn't stick out in the normal world, but she still managed to look out of place.

"What are you doing here?" Fiona repeated.

"Waiting to talk to Wynn's friend. And you?"

"Watching. It's my turn."

"Your turn to watch what?"

Fiona nodded toward the van. "We've been taking turns watching the campsite. I'm quite proud of the hiding spot I found. You didn't even notice me. Anyway, something is off about these two."

"You mean Wynn and Claw?"

"After Wynn treated Seraphina so badly, I asked around and found out where he was working. I was heading to the diner when Gunnar hollered at me Friday night. I wanted to have a little chat with Wynn about boundaries and respect."

"And?" I prompted.

"And I got to the diner, but he wasn't there. He had gotten off work earlier. So, I started to head toward the saloon, thinking maybe he had gone there for a drink. But he wasn't there, either." A sad, high-pitched whine escaped Fiona's lips. "He was killed before I could threaten to kill him."

"That's a shame."

Fiona didn't seem to notice my sarcasm, because she said, "Thank you. But this companion, there's something strange about him, too. We've been shadowing him a bit, but mostly, we keep tabs on him here."

"What has he done that's strange?"

"He hasn't actually done anything. It's the aura he gives off."

His vibes, then. Just like Mama and Lucy sensing there was something off about Cowan. What was with the creepy people arriving in Nightmare lately?

"Come on," Fiona said. "We shouldn't be sitting out here. We're too obvious."

I glanced at her dress, then at my shorts and tank top. "I'm not."

Fiona took my hand and stood. "Come."

Reluctantly, I followed her to a cluster of tall bushes. Fiona deftly slid through a break in the foliage, and I followed to find myself in a small hollow place in the middle of the bushes. It wasn't very roomy, but we were hidden from all directions. "No wonder I didn't see you," I commented.

We stood there for about twenty minutes before I asked Fiona how long her watch would last. She glanced up at the sun. "About another ninety minutes."

We continued to wait. I couldn't tell the time by the sun

like Fiona could, but a glance at my watch showed me I had only been at the campground for forty-five minutes. I was getting tired of standing in one spot, and some tiny bugs had discovered my ankles. I scratched at one ankle while hopping on one foot. I was just considering giving up when someone walked into view, heading right for the van.

It was Jeff Crosley.

"What?" I whispered. Fiona elbowed me and shot me a look that clearly demanded I remain silent.

Jeff walked right up to the van and knocked, just as I had. While he waited, he looked around nervously. It was almost like he knew he was being watched, and even though Fiona and I were well hidden, I shrank back and ducked my head when Jeff's eyes roved in our direction.

When I had seen Jeff and Cowan in the alley earlier, they seemed to know each other. That had been strange enough, but Jeff seemed to know Claw, too. I had discounted Jeff as a suspect after what Ross had said about him, but I was going to have to rethink that.

Hang on. Don't jump to conclusions, I told myself. Of course Jeff and Claw knew each other. Jeff had hired Wynn, who had then been murdered at Jeff's diner. It was inevitable Jeff and Claw would have met each other in the aftermath of that, probably at the police station.

That meant Jeff might be able to give me some insight about Claw, and whether or not it was worth my time to keep waiting for him to show up. "I'm going to talk to him," I whispered to Fiona.

She grabbed my arm and mouthed, "No."

I peered through the branches and saw Jeff beginning to walk away. As soon as he had disappeared from our line of sight, Fiona let go of my arm. I instantly shot out of our hiding place and sprinted in the direction Jeff had been walking.

Jeff wasn't that far away, and he turned when he heard

me running up behind him. He raised his arms ever so slightly, like he was preparing to fight off an attacker if needed. When he saw me, he lowered his arms, and his stance relaxed. "Hello," he said cautiously.

"Hi." I hadn't run far, but I was out of shape, so I took a couple of shallow breaths before I could continue. "I'm Olivia. We met the other night."

"Did we?"

Oops. I had forgotten Jeff had been under Mori's influence when we had visited him in his office. There was no way he remembered me, let alone that entire encounter, since he had been mesmerized.

"Oh, well, I come into the diner a lot, at any rate," I said to cover my gaffe.

"I know. I've seen you. You're new in town, and you work at Nightmare Sanctuary."

Wow, Nightmare really is a small town. It was strange how many people knew me and my business. "Yeah. I'm trying to help Ella."

Jeff smiled at me sadly. "She needs all the help she can get. I believed it was her when I first saw her on the security camera footage, but now I think there's more to the story."

"What made you change your mind about Ella?"

Jeff hesitated. "It just seems too perfect, doesn't it? Ella knows full well where the security cameras are, but she didn't even try to hide her face from them. If she was really going to the diner to kill someone, she would have disguised herself better and taken a route that avoided the cameras. I think someone doctored that video."

"I think so, too. And since you're here, I'm guessing that means you think Claw might have done it."

Jeff balked at me. "Claw? No, of course not. Why would he have killed his best friend? We're actually working together to find Wynn's killer."

"How do you know it wasn't Claw? He could be leading you on."

"I don't believe that."

"But—" I stopped myself as I saw someone hurrying up behind Jeff. It was a guy who looked like he was in his late twenties. His brown hair was clipped short, and his tanned face had a scar across the left cheek. He looked almost sinister.

Jeff turned around when he saw my focus shift. "Speak of the devil," he said in a friendly tone.

Claw, on the other hand, sounded wary as he eyed me. "Everything okay, Jeff?"

"Yeah, we're fine. Claw, meet Olivia. She also thinks Ella was framed."

Claw looked me up and down, then nodded at me curtly. "Good. The more people we have working on this, the better." Despite his welcoming words, he still spoke as if he didn't quite trust me. I couldn't blame him. The feeling was mutual.

"Let's discuss this in the van," Claw said, his eyes darting around the campground. "I feel like we're being watched."

You're not wrong, I thought. Jeff and Claw might trust each other, but they certainly didn't trust anyone else.

I guess I looked uncertain—I was definitely feeling that way—because Jeff put a gentle hand on my shoulder and peered at me earnestly. "It's okay, Olivia. You can trust Claw."

"Look, I want to help Ella, and I believe you want the same," I said. "But you're asking me to trust a total stranger when there is a killer on the loose in Nightmare." I glanced at Claw. "Sorry. It's nothing personal."

Claw looked more impressed than offended. "Your caution is warranted. If Wynn had been more cautious, he might still be alive."

"Wynn's behavior was questionable," I noted, "and not just in the caution department. I can see how the way he treated people made him a target." I opened my mouth to say more, but Claw gestured subtly for me to wait. His focus was on something behind me, and I turned my head slightly to see a woman in shorts and hiking boots walking along, a water bottle in one hand.

"The longer we stand out here, the more we risk becoming a target," Jeff said tersely, as soon as the woman had passed out of earshot. "I'm with Claw. I feel like we're being watched."

Even though I knew who was watching us and that we were in zero danger, I still felt a little shiver run up my back as I glanced at the trees and underbrush around us. *Fiona may not be the only one watching*, I realized.

Jeff took a step in the direction of the van and reached toward me, his fingers stopping just before they touched my arm. "Please, Olivia. We need to get inside. There's more going on here than you realize, and I don't like being out in the open. Wynn was the son of my best friend. Well, my former best friend. He was murdered, too."

CHAPTER FOURTEEN

I gaped at Jeff, and he nodded grimly. "Like I said, I think this is about more than just one murder. Come on in the van, and I'll explain everything."

As Claw and Jeff led the way to the camper van, I looked toward the cluster of bushes where Fiona and I had been hiding. I tried to make a facial expression that said, "*Everything is okay, and I'm not in trouble*," so Fiona would know I wasn't going inside with two suspects against my will. Because in my mind, Jeff and Claw were still suspects, but I was willing to hear them out.

And I really, really hoped they were not killers. The last thing I wanted was to be in a confined space with violent criminals.

When we got to the van, Claw unlocked the sliding side door. Instead of letting it open all the way, though, he opened it just wide enough to poke his head inside. Then he looked back at me and smiled apologetically. "Give me thirty seconds. I wasn't expecting company."

Claw disappeared inside the van, shutting the door behind him. Just as he had promised, though, he soon opened the door all the way and swept one arm grandly. "Welcome to my home! Come on in."

The van had been converted into a camper. There was

a twin bed against the back doors, a tiny kitchen area that made my own look like something from a mansion, and a cramped sofa that, judging by the pillow on it, doubled as a bed.

Claw settled cross-legged onto a small patch of tan carpet. As Jeff and I sat on the sofa, my eyes glanced around and landed on something long and metallic poking up between the sofa and a cabinet. It had a sharp end, like an arrowhead. In fact, it looked exactly like a spear. The shaft had something carved into it, and I leaned forward to squint at it.

I was still staring at the strange object when Claw said, "Fire poker. We cook... *I* cook most of my food over the campfire."

It did not look like any fire poker I had ever seen. Maybe Claw killed his own food before he cooked it, and he stabbed it with that spear. Still, I didn't want to be rude, so I turned my attention back to him just as Jeff said, "Olivia helped solve a murder a few weeks ago. Having her with us might be valuable."

"Jeff, I'm sorry your best friend was murdered," I said, "but why do you think it's related to Wynn's murder?"

Jeff's jaw worked for a moment, and he stared at a dark stain on the carpet. "Brandon was a good man. We knew each other for nearly twenty years, and I considered him a brother. He and I were on a camping trip once,"—Jeff gestured toward Claw—"not unlike Wynn and Claw, and Brandon kept getting this feeling like we were being watched. One day, when I woke up, Brandon wasn't there. I figured he was just up early, so I went outside, expecting him to be having coffee or getting in some exercise. He wasn't there, though. I searched for two hours, and I finally found him about half a mile from our campsite. He was face down in a creek."

"Was he drowned, too?" I asked, horrified. The similarity to Wynn's death wasn't lost on me, though I had to remind myself Wynn had also been stabbed.

Jeff shrugged. "It's possible something caused him to go unconscious, and he just so happened to fall into the water. There was no autopsy, so we'll never know for sure."

I frowned. "What made you think it was murder, then? He could have slipped and hit his head."

Jeff finally tore his eyes away from the spot on the carpet and looked at me. "You're right. That could have been the case, except for one thing. Brandon had a notebook, a journal of sorts. It was filled with personal information, so he had everything he needed no matter where he was in the world." Jeff smiled sadly. "Brandon wasn't the type to stay in one place for a long time, and he never felt the need to own a lot of possessions. His notebook, a few changes of clothes, and some camping gear were all he needed.

"I knew there was nothing I could do for Brandon. He was cold by the time I found him. But he had always told me that if something happened to him, he wanted me to take the notebook for safekeeping. The problem was, I couldn't find it anywhere. Not at the campsite, and not on Brandon. It was gone."

"Maybe it floated down the river," I suggested gently.

"Sure. And his wallet slipped out of his pocket, dumped all the cash that was in it, and put itself back into his pocket. He was killed for about thirty bucks."

That little detail did make it sound like Brandon had been murdered, but I still didn't see how it had anything to do with Wynn's death, other than the fact both of them landed face-first into a body of water. Claw saved me the effort of asking, saying, "Brandon's killer was never found. Shortly after we arrived in Nightmare, Wynn started getting the feeling like he was being watched. He had heard the stories about his dad's death, so it rattled him. We told Jeff about it, and he agreed to keep an eye out. Frankly, we expected that if anyone was going to come after Wynn, it would be here, at the campsite, not in the diner."

"You gave Wynn a job because you'd been friends with his dad," I said to Jeff.

"And because I wanted to keep an eye on him. He was a good kid. He didn't deserve this."

The similarities between the deaths of father and son still seemed coincidental to me. Copper Creek Campground was beautiful, but I could see how one might imagine unseen eyes in a secluded spot like that. It was possible Wynn and Claw had been jumping at shadows.

"Now I need to get a job so I can afford to get out of this town," Claw said.

"I said the exact same thing just about a month ago, when I got to Nightmare," I said with a small laugh. "Watch out, or you'll wind up deciding you like it here and don't want to leave."

"No, I'm definitely going to move on once I get some cash. I'm thinking about asking if that haunted house on the edge of town is looking for help. I feel like I might be a good fit there."

Alarm bells started going off in my head. That was almost verbatim what Cowan had said to me. Had Cowan arrived in town the same week as Wynn and Claw because they were planning to meet up with Jeff here in Nightmare? Maybe Cowan, Jeff, and Claw had turned on Wynn for some reason. Even though they were claiming their innocence, maybe they were just trying to throw me—and the police—off their trail.

I really needed to work on my trust issues. Another thing I blamed my ex for.

I was done with speculation. Before I could start an internal debate about whether or not it was a smart idea, I said, "So, how do the two of you know Cowan Rhodes?"

Jeff and Claw both jerked backward slightly. They stared at me, then turned and stared at each other. It was Jeff who finally spoke. "You don't want to get involved with Cowan."

"Why, because he might threaten me with a giant knife?" I raised my eyebrows at Jeff.

"Exactly. Cowan sometimes acts before he thinks. I promise you, he wants to find Wynn's killer, too, but you don't need to talk to him directly."

In other words, Cowan was—allegedly—on our side, but he was dangerous. Mama had been right to be wary of him. Even if he turned out to be innocent of murder, that didn't mean he was a good man.

"It might be tough to avoid him, since I live right above his motel room," I said. "Still, I'll steer clear of him."

I wasn't going to make any promises, though.

Jeff looked at his watch. "I think it's time for dinner. We could all use a break. Olivia, would you like to join us? I'm thinking Mexican."

"Thanks, but I'm going to head home. I appreciate you trusting me enough to tell me about Brandon."

"Now you understand why I'm so anxious to find Wynn's killer. Not only did it happen at my diner, but it happened to my best friend's son."

The three of us emerged from the van, and I was startled to realize the sun was just slipping below the mountains on the horizon. No wonder Jeff was thinking about dinner. I said my goodbyes to him and Claw, and we parted ways. I had parked in a different area, so I headed toward my car, then ducked behind a tree. I waited for what I figured was a sufficient amount of time, then crept back to Claw's campsite. I didn't head for the van, though.

Instead, I made a beeline for the bushes where I knew Fiona was hiding.

Except it wasn't just Fiona. Malcolm and Zach were there, too.

"We were going to rip the door off that van and come get you if you'd been in there much longer," Malcolm said in greeting.

Instead of answering him, I looked at Fiona questioningly. She straightened her shoulders and said, "I called for backup when you ran after that man. He could have hurt you. Or worse."

She wasn't wrong, but I relayed what Jeff had said about Wynn's father. Zach agreed the murders probably weren't connected, but he added, "At least now I understand why you were willing to hear him out. If he really does believe Ella was framed, then his help can only be good for her."

"Exactly." I realized I was eyeing Zach stubbornly, and I forced myself to relax. I was getting defensive for no reason. "I appreciate all of you looking out for me."

"You just joined our family," Malcolm said. "We're not about to let you get hurt."

"There was one strange thing," I said. I told them about the metal arrow or spike or whatever it was that Claw had said was a poker for the campfire. I finished with, "Not only do I not believe Claw about it being a fire poker, but there was also something carved in the shaft. I don't think it was writing, though. Not English, at any rate."

"I wouldn't mind getting a closer look," Zach said. He looked like he was ready to jump right through the bushes to get to the van faster.

Malcolm put out a hand. "I would like that, as well, but we're not the ones who can gain access to a place without breaking locks or smashing windows. I suggest we leave this job to our resident ghosts."

CHAPTER FIFTEEN

"You mean Tanner and McCrory?" I asked incredulously.

"Of course," Malcolm said. "They might have killed each other in a shootout, but these days, they make a pretty good team. I'm sure they'd be happy to help us."

The first time I had seen the ghosts of the two cowboys, they had glided right through a wall. I could see why Malcolm thought they were our best bet for getting a look at that spear.

"Let's get them now," I suggested. "We're all off work tonight since the haunt is closed, and Claw is at dinner with Jeff. If we hurry, we can get back here so the ghosts can take a look around before Claw returns."

It was Malcolm's turn to be on watch at the campsite, so Fiona and Zach were heading back to the Sanctuary. Zach was driving a beat-up blue truck, but Fiona asked to ride with me since I was following in my car. "I like air-conditioning," Fiona explained. "We didn't have it when I lived in Ireland, but then again, it didn't get so hot there."

It only took us about fifteen minutes to get to the Sanctuary. As soon as the three of us walked through the front doors, Fiona began to wail. I clamped my hands over my ears and felt tears spring to my eyes. Her tone rose and fell, but it always stayed at a painfully high pitch.

When Fiona fell silent again, I asked in a quaking voice, "Are you done?"

"Oh, I should have warned you. That's how I call Tanner and McCrory."

Sure enough, the two cowboys were floating down the staircase. Butch Tanner had apparently been an outlaw back in the late eighteen hundreds, when Nightmare was a booming copper mining town. He wore a red bandana over his nose and mouth, and his tan duster floated in a nonexistent wind. Connor McCrory wore a black duster over his white shirt and black trousers, and he had a matching black cowboy hat. Even though he looked like some kind of Wild West villain, complete with a big bushy mustache, I knew from seeing a reenactment of the shootout that McCrory had been the lawman trying to keep Nightmare safe.

"Hello, Miss Fiona," McCrory said as he came to a stop in front of us. "Zach. Ma'am."

I giggled, partly from nerves and partly from being addressed so formally. And by a ghost, no less. "You can call me Olivia. It's nice to meet you both."

Tanner winked at me and pulled down his bandana for just a moment, revealing a tanned, weather-beaten face. He had a cleft in his chin and a mischievous smile. "Nice to meet you, Miss Olivia."

"We need your help, if you're willing," Fiona said. "Olivia is trying to clear a friend of hers from murder charges."

McCrory's lips turned down under his dark mustache. "Do you think your friend has been falsely accused?" he asked me.

"I do. There's some evidence to suggest she killed the new dishwasher at The Lusty Lunch Counter, but several of us believe the evidence was faked in order to make her look guilty."

"And where do we come in?" Tanner asked eagerly. "Do we get to haunt the person you think really did the killing? We can make them so miserable they'd rather confess and spend a lifetime in jail."

"No, nothing like that," I said, waving my hands. "In fact, I'm having a hard time pinning down a suspect. Everyone seems to have a reason why they couldn't have been the killer. However, I saw something curious today, and I'd sure appreciate it if you two would have another look." I quickly explained my meeting with Jeff and Claw, and I described the spear I had seen.

McCrory's mouth tightened. "I don't normally condone breaking into someone's private property."

"Oh, come on, McCrory. We're just going to look around. We're not going to steal anything." Even though the bandana covered his mouth, I just knew Tanner was grinning. "I haven't broken into a stagecoach in over a hundred years. This will be fun!"

"Olivia and I will take you now," Zach said. "We don't have much time."

"Just grab our guns, and we'll be ready to go," McCrory said.

"You won't need to shoot anyone," I clarified.

"I know that, Miss Olivia, but we need our guns none-theless. Some ghosts are tethered to a location, like the place where they died. Tanner and I are tethered to our six-shooters. Where they go, we go."

"It's a good thing a collector kept them after the shootout," Zach said casually. "Otherwise, who knows where these two would have ended up? I'll go get them from Baxter's office."

"Damien's office," Fiona and I said in unison. Fiona made a little gagging noise afterward, so I knew she disliked the idea as much as I did.

I gave Tanner and McCrory a few more details while

we waited. It was just a few minutes before Zach rejoined us, but Damien stepped up right next to him, and he didn't look happy at all. I didn't know what excuse he would have for why we couldn't take the ghosts to the campground, but I knew it was coming.

Which was why I was stunned when Damien said, "I'm going with Olivia." It was only then I noticed Damien was carrying a dark wooden box in his hands. The box looked old, and there were chips on the corners. A small padlock was fastened on the latch. The box was just the right size for two six-shooters.

"Why you?" I asked.

"I'm only here right now because I was looking for you." Damien leveled a look at me that made me feel like I was a kid who had broken curfew. "Mama couldn't find you, and you don't have a cell phone. She called me in a panic, worried something bad had happened to you. Where have you been?"

"Talking to suspects at the campground." I gestured toward Tanner and McCrory. "That's why we need their help."

Damien sighed. "Mama has every right to be worried about you."

"You can lecture me on the drive. But we need to get this done before Claw gets back from dinner, so let's go." I pointed myself in the direction of the front doors and started walking. Luckily, Damien didn't argue. Instead, he slid on his mirrored sunglasses and followed.

Zach wished me good luck as we headed outside. I climbed into my car and glanced at my rearview mirror just in time to see the two ghosts float through the doors into the back seat. I had to fight the urge to stare at them in my rearview mirror as I started the car. Giving ghosts a ride around town was not something I ever thought I would do.

I filled Damien in on what we were doing. Once I told him about the spear with the mysterious symbols on it, he seemed less gruff and more curious. He instructed me to park down a narrow side road shortly before we reached the entrance to Copper Creek Campground. "We'll be a little less obvious if we walk in," Damien explained. "Don't stop driving until you go around the curve. I don't want your car to be visible from the main road."

For someone who claimed to be against this venture, Damien sure was taking charge. Still, I did as he instructed, and soon, we were walking down a footpath that paralleled the road.

When we got close to Claw's campsite, Damien put out an arm. "You and I will stay here, where we're less likely to be noticed. Tanner and McCrory, you two go on ahead. We should be close enough that you can reach the van."

I pointed out exactly which campsite was Claw's, and the ghosts took off. Once they got a short distance away, I could no longer see them. While we waited for them to go inside the van and get a look around, I turned to Damien and said, "What are you more afraid of: that I'll get into trouble, or that Mama will yell at you if I get into trouble?"

"She caught me smoking when I was sixteen. I was behind a convenience store with some friends, and she came storming back there and started yelling. I've been mildly terrified of her ever since."

The idea of a teenage Damien getting a lecture from Mama was thoroughly amusing to me, and I laughed.

A small smile spread over Damien's face. "She's a good woman. I have a lot of respect for her. And, for some reason, she's decided to take you under her wing. You should be grateful."

I nodded vigorously. "Oh, I am, believe me. If she hadn't loaned me her granddaughter's phone, I wouldn't have been able to ask for help when Luke Dawes came after me. I'd be… Well, I wouldn't be standing here right now. Plus, she's made me feel welcome here. Like everyone at the Sanctuary. They make me feel like I belong."

I had not expected to say something so honest and personal to Damien. He slowly pulled off his sunglasses and stared at me for a quiet moment. It was a look he had given me a few times before, like I was a puzzle he was trying to solve. "You do belong," he said softly. "I wish I knew what that felt like."

I couldn't believe Damien was actually opening up to me. For once, I didn't return his curious stare with my own glare of defiance. "Do you really resent the Sanctuary that much for keeping you from living in the normal Nightmare?"

"It's not about that," Damien began right as an icy cold enveloped my left shoulder. I looked over in surprise and saw McCrory standing close to me, his hand hovering over my arm like he wanted to grab it. Tanner stood just behind him, but he was looking over his shoulder, toward Claw's van.

"There's iron in his wagon," McCrory said. "Too much for us."

I tilted my head. "What's wrong with iron?"

"Iron is used to ward off ghosts and some other super-natural beings," Damien answered. "Ghosts can't cross a large concentration of iron."

"Boss man is right," McCrory said. "Whatever that boy's wagon is made from, we can't get in."

"The van should be made of steel, like other vehicles." I frowned. "I wonder if something inside is constructed of iron."

"Even if that mysterious spear you saw was made from iron, it wouldn't be enough to keep us from at least getting a look at it." McCrory turned and looked in the same direction as Tanner, whose right hand hovered near his waist. He felt threatened, I supposed, and out of habit, his fingers were inching ever closer to his holster.

Tanner kept his gaze fixed on the van, but even with his back to us, I could clearly hear him say, "It's like that stagecoach is warded against us."

CHAPTER SIXTEEN

"Do you think Claw and Wynn really warded their van against ghosts?" I asked.

"Probably not," McCrory said, "but Tanner always likes to think the worst of people. You should ask him what he used to think of me!"

Tanner muttered something under his breath. All I caught was "law-abidin' folk" and something about whiskey.

Since the ghosts couldn't get inside Claw's van, there was no point sticking around. We made our way back to my car, and then I had the difficult job of getting it turned around on such a narrow dirt road. It took a lot of back and forth, but eventually, we were on our way back to the Sanctuary.

On the way, we passed the old mine Gunnar and I had walked past on Thursday night. When I mentioned the voice I had heard, it gave me a thought. "Gentlemen," I said, glancing at Tanner and McCrory in my rearview mirror, "would you like to try getting into that old mine we just drove past? Gunnar and I passed it the other night, and I distinctly heard a voice coming from it. It was a man's voice saying, 'My ashes are my own.' I'm curious to know how someone got inside the mine even though the entrance is locked up."

"Sure, we'd be happy to," McCrory said affably. "That used to be Sonny Dickinson's mine, but I don't know whose it is now. I suppose it stopped giving copper a long time ago, like the big mine."

"Later," Damien said. He had returned to his gruff demeanor shortly after beginning to open up to me, and I knew there was no way he was going to take his sunglasses off again on this trip. "It's getting too dark, Olivia, and you shouldn't be out exploring a mine when there's a murderer on the loose."

When we got back to the Sanctuary, we found Zach, Fiona, and Seraphina in the dining room. Theo and Mori came in just a few minutes after we did, and everyone was soon caught up on the uneventful trip. By then, I was feeling drained from such a long afternoon, so I wished everyone a good night and began my walk out.

I was halfway down the hall before I realized Damien was right on my heels. When we reached the entryway, he said abruptly, "Do I need to keep watch over you again, like I did when Jared's killer was still on the loose and threatening you?"

I turned slowly and looked at Damien curiously. "Do you think I'm in danger from Wynn's killer?"

Damien's fingers tightened on the wooden box containing the six-shooters. "No. I think you might be in danger from yourself."

I huffed out a breath. "Damien, if this is about me wanting to help clear Ella's name—"

"It's about what you heard at the mine. You said you were with Gunnar at the time. Did he hear it, too?"

"No, Gunnar didn't hear the voice at all. I don't see how that makes me dangerous, to myself or to anyone else."

"You heard a voice so clearly that you understood every word, but Gunnar didn't hear anything at all."

"I had my ear up to the door the second time," I pointed out.

"Did it not occur to you that what you heard could be related to your conjuring skills?"

I peered at Damien's face, looking for any sign that he was joking. "How could the two things possibly be related? You believe I want so badly for things to happen that I make them happen, but I never wanted to hear a voice from the mine."

"But you want to find my father, don't you?"

"Of course. You know I want to help find Baxter."

"Those words you heard? My father used to say them. I think you're somehow connected to him. It was his handwriting on the job listing you found, after you realized you desperately needed work, and now you're hearing his voice." Damien was clutching the box so hard his knuckles were white.

"You think I want to find Baxter so badly that I'm somehow... What? Channeling him?"

"I don't know."

"What did his words even mean? 'My ashes are my own' makes no sense to me."

"I don't know that, either. He would say that whenever he felt like his authority was being threatened, but he would never explain it to me."

Justine came through the front doors at that moment. She brightened and said hello, then her feet faltered. She seemed to sense there was an intense conversation happening, and she scooted past us and disappeared down the hall without another word.

"Let's go to your office," I suggested. I didn't want anyone to overhear Damien's theories about me, and I was worried Damien would get splinters if he didn't relax his grip on the box.

Once we were inside Damien's office with the door

closed, I said, "You're telling me the voice I heard coming from the mine was your father's. That doesn't mean I have any kind of supernatural power. In fact, I think it might mean your dad is inside that mine. Maybe he's being held captive in there."

"Tanner and McCrory will find out soon enough," Damien answered dismissively.

"Soon enough? Baxter has been missing for six months! If there's a chance he's in that mine, shouldn't we go right now?" I knew Damien and his dad had a strained relationship, but I was appalled he didn't want to drop everything and go look for Baxter that very moment.

"Honestly, I don't think we'll find him there. If he had been so close to the Sanctuary this whole time, someone here would have found out. One of our psychic mediums would have sensed him, or the clairvoyant would have seen him in a vision." When I opened my mouth to protest, Damien stopped me with, "But I do want to check the mine out. Let's see what Tanner and McCrory find. How early do you want to go tomorrow?"

"I'll pick them up at eight."

"No, I'll pick you up at that time, and I'll have them with me. I'll see you tomorrow."

There was a note of finality in Damien's voice, so I gave him a nod and headed out. I drove back to the motel, thinking over all the strange revelations of the day. Jeff had known Wynn's father, Wynn and Claw had a van that was impervious to ghosts, and the voice I had heard in the mine had been Baxter's. Or, at any rate, the phrase had been Baxter's. It was entirely possible I had heard someone else saying the same words.

Either way, it only made me even more curious to know what was inside that mine, and how people had gotten in there. Unlike Damien, I did not want to wait until the next morning to find out. On the other hand, I also agreed with his logic about waiting for daylight. Gunnar had warned me about running into a cactus if I went traipsing around the mine at night, and Damien had warned me about running into a murderer in the same scenario. Both of them made good points, so I cooked dinner, ate, and went to bed.

I had suggested an eight o'clock departure for the mine because I was so eager to learn its secrets. I hadn't taken my new nocturnal lifestyle into the equation, and when the alarm went off at seven, I instantly regretted my decision. I got my coffee maker started and threw on navy-blue shorts and a white sleeveless blouse. It was a little fancy for exploring an old mine, but Tanner and McCrory would be the ones actually going inside it, so I didn't have to worry about getting dirty.

While the coffee was percolating, I dashed up to the front office to check in with Mama. I had stopped by the night before, too, to reassure her I was safe and to apologize for having worried her. This time, I told her I was going to explore the area around an old mine with Damien. I didn't explain why, and Mama didn't ask. Instead, she got a little smile on her face and told me to enjoy the adventure. She seemed to like the idea of me spending more time with Damien, almost as much as I disliked the idea.

I got back to my apartment and hastily had some coffee and a bagel, then I gave my hair a quick brush. I put sunscreen on my face but didn't bother with makeup. I wasn't trying to impress anyone I would be seeing that morning.

Damien arrived promptly at eight, with Tanner and McCrory sitting in the back seat of his silver Corvette. It was a tight squeeze for them, but I guessed it really didn't matter to ghosts with no corporeal bodies. I slid into the passenger seat and said good morning. In answer, Tanner let out a whistle. "Modern women," he drawled, eyeing my bare legs appreciatively.

When we arrived at the mine, Damien pulled his car over to the side of the road. The box containing the six-shooters was sitting at my feet, so I grabbed it and hopped out. I could feel the cold radiating from the ghosts as they followed me to the rusty door, even though I could barely see them in the bright daylight. Just a light shimmer in the air indicated where they were. "Take a look and let me know what you see inside, please," I told them.

"This door is lined with iron," McCrory said. "Probably for extra security. We'll try going through the side of the hill."

I waited, staring at the door, while the two of them headed off. Damien eventually joined me. "We could just wait in the car, you know," he said. "No point standing out here in the heat."

"I thought maybe I'd hear the voice again," I answered.

Damien curled his fingers around the old lock. "No one has used this entrance in ages."

"And we can't find any other way in." McCrory's voice came from behind us. "It's not just the door that's lined with iron. It's the whole mine. We could pass into the hill itself, then *bam*! Solid iron. Top, bottom, and sides. Someone took a lot of measures to keep ghosts out of this mine."

"Why?" Damien and I asked in unison.

"I don't know, but I'm sorry we can't help you yet again, Miss Olivia."

"I appreciate you trying, though. Damien will take you back to the Sanctuary. I'm going to walk over to the real estate office to ask Emmett what he knows about this mine."

"Do you think that's safe? I can go with you," Damien said.

I waved a hand. "I'm not afraid of Emmett. Not anymore, at least. I'll be fine."

"Be careful, and let me know what you learn," Damien instructed.

I gave him a little salute, thanked the ghosts again, and started walking in the direction of Emmett's office.

Emmett was just unlocking the front door when I arrived. He seemed surprised to see me, but he waved me inside with a smile. "I didn't expect to see you again so soon. Do you have more questions about the dishwasher?"

"No. Actually, I was hoping you might help me find the owner of a piece of property. An old mine about halfway between here and Nightmare Sanctuary."

"Sure. That information is public record, but it would be faster for me to look it up than to explain to you how to do it yourself." Emmett produced a map of Nightmare from a desk drawer. He spread it out across the desk and told me to point out exactly where the mine was.

I found it fairly easily. It was labeled *Sonny's Folly*.

Emmett moved behind his desk, sat down, and began typing away on a laptop. After a few moments, he sat back and said, "Isn't that interesting."

"What?" I asked, leaning over the desk to look at his screen.

"Sonny's Folly Mine was sold in nineteen sixty-three. It is currently owned by Baxter Shackleford."

CHAPTER SEVENTEEN

"Baxter?" I repeated. "Damien's father? The guy who owns the Sanctuary?"

"I can't imagine there's anyone else in the world with that name, let alone here in Nightmare," Emmett said with a laugh.

I started running numbers in my head. Would Baxter have been old enough to buy a mine back in sixty-three? Damien was about my age, forty-two, so his dad was probably in his sixties. I thought back to a photo I had seen of Baxter in a Sanctuary photo album. Madge had shown it to me, and she had mentioned the photo was around forty years old. In the photo, Baxter had looked like he was in his fifties. If Baxter had been in his fifties when the photo had been taken forty years ago, that would make him around ninety when he went missing.

That didn't seem right. Everyone spoke about Baxter as if he were a lot younger than that. I wondered if Madge had gotten the timeframe of the photo wrong. Or, maybe, Baxter was far older than I had assumed.

Emmett was looking at me curiously. "Olivia? Is it significant that Baxter owns the mine?"

"Maybe," I said honestly.

"I didn't even know. When I was trying to get him to sell the old hospital building to me, it never occurred to me that he might own other properties around town. I wonder what he wanted with an old mine."

"I hope to find that out. Is there any way of looking into what else he might own around here?"

Emmett smiled. "I'm willing to do a little digging. And like I've said, I owe you one for clearing my name in Jared's murder. I've got some work I need to get done first, but when I have a chance, I'll take a look. Give me about a week."

I thanked Emmett profusely for his help, then headed back to my apartment. During the walk, I asked myself over and over why Baxter, who provided a safe haven for supernatural creatures, would have a mine that was warded against ghosts. Was he hiding some kind of secret in there?

For once, I was looking forward to talking to Damien, because I wanted to know what he made of this news.

By the time I drove to the Sanctuary for work that night, I was feeling defeated. I couldn't get a handle on who might have framed Ella and killed Wynn, and Baxter was becoming more mysterious by the day.

I was pleased when Justine told me during the family meeting that I would be in the abandoned hospital vignette again that night. With so much going on, focusing on scaring guests would be a great way to turn off my brain for a while. Before long, I was dressed in a ratty hospital gown that had red splatters all over it. I was wearing a long, tangled brown wig, and I had put makeup on my face to look like I was mostly dead.

About an hour before closing, I was trying to hide my smile as a couple practically sprinted out of the vignette in fear. I had stepped in front of them at exactly the right moment. My quiet laugh turned into a shout of surprise when Madge popped out of a door marked *Surgery*. It led into the network of paths between vignettes that let us come and go unseen.

Madge's words came out in a rush. "He's here! He's here! It's him!"

I took one of Madge's hands. "Who's here?"

"Robert! Ugh, I mean Cowan! And I don't think he's here just to enjoy the haunt." Madge threw a nervous glance toward the group of guests just entering the scene.

"Where is he now?"

"He was just in the cemetery, so he's coming this way. Fiona saw him. She's gone to get help."

Before I could ask why Fiona was going for help, Morgan and Maida filed through the door, and the three witches looked so incredibly out of place in the hospital vignette that I would have laughed if Madge hadn't been so upset.

"He's ready for battle with those who are like us," Morgan said. She had pulled her diminutive body to its fullest height, and there was a defiant look on her wrinkled face.

"He carries a silver knife and an iron rod, and he wears a four-leaf clover around his neck," Maida added.

"He's armed?" I didn't know the significance of the knife being silver, but it must be dangerous for some kind of supernatural creature. He was carrying weapons that could hurt my friends. That meant Cowan must know the secret of the Sanctuary, and he was looking for trouble.

The guests who had walked into the scene were staring at us uncertainly. Suddenly, the man at the back of the group yelped loudly. He spread his arms and pushed the other three people ahead of him as he hustled past us and out of the vignette.

I tensed, expecting to see Cowan standing where the guests had just been. Beside me, Madge did the same. She dropped my hand, and her arms rose as her fingers spread. I suspected she was preparing to put a spell on Cowan.

Except it wasn't Cowan standing there. It was Theo, and he looked ready for a fight. "First a van with too much iron for our ghosts, and now a guest who's armed for supernatural battle. These aren't coincidences. These men are hunters."

The three witches gasped and made noises of dismay, but I asked, "Hunters?"

"Monster hunters," Theo said.

It had never occurred to me that if supernatural creatures were real, then so were the stories about the people who went after them. The idea anyone would want to hurt my friends was horrifying. "But you're not monsters," I argued.

"We are to some," Theo said sadly. "And there are those among our kind who truly are monsters. You think all vampires would make you a friend instead of a meal?"

I hadn't thought about that scenario, and I instinctively put a hand over my neck.

"He'll be here soon," Morgan said. "I can feel him coming."

"But you can throw him out, Mister Theo," Maida said. Her eyes were wide, and I wondered how monster hunters felt about supernatural children. Would Cowan go after Maida if he had a chance?

"No," Madge said firmly. "It's too dangerous. We'll follow him, and I'll hit him with a sleeping hex the second he makes a move."

Theo turned and headed back in the direction he had come from, toward the lagoon vignette. Before he had gone two steps, Madge jumped forward and grabbed his arm. "And please don't hurt him!"

"I can't promise that," Theo grumbled.

The witches and I fell into line behind Theo. We had

completely abandoned trying to entertain guests, and I expected the same was true in most of the vignettes throughout the haunt. Damien would probably lecture us about it at the next family meeting, but at the moment, it didn't matter. My friends were in danger.

We had just reached the edge of the vignette when Theo stopped short. Cowan was emerging from the dark hallway that connected the lagoon and hospital vignettes. He had a metal rod about two feet long in his left hand, and his right hand was curled around a silver knife that was tucked into his belt. He must have kept those items hidden when he bought his ticket and entered the Sanctuary, then pulled them out as soon as he was in the dark hallway at the beginning of the haunted house.

Cowan planted his feet and faced Theo defiantly. His eyes twitched in Madge's direction, and he said in a low voice, "I don't want to hurt you."

"Then why did you show up armed?" Theo countered. He took a small, slow step closer to Cowan.

"Because you're harboring a killer here." Cowan raised his right hand, and I saw a flash of silver. He had the knife gripped tightly.

Theo seemed undaunted, because he took another step toward Cowan. "I don't know if you're brave or stupid. You showed up here, alone, to accuse one of us of murder."

This time, Cowan stepped backward. "I'm only interested in the killer. I don't plan to hurt anyone else."

"You're not going to hurt anyone," a voice growled from the darkness of the hallway. Cowan whirled around, raising the knife even higher. Madge cried out as Theo quickly stepped forward to close the gap between himself and Cowan, who was effectively trapped.

At first, I couldn't see anyone in the hallway. As I stared into the darkness, though, I saw two small green orbs.

They shifted slightly, then Damien came into view. His eyes glowed with an inner light. I had seen his eyes glow before, but it had been a quick flash that I thought I might have imagined. There was no doubt, this time. Damien was definitely supernatural. Zach was just behind Damien, his shoulders rounded forward, and his lips pulled back to show his teeth.

Cowan brought the knife down, and Damien's eyes flashed so brightly I had to shut my own against the light.

I heard someone cry out, and when I opened my eyes again, Zach had Cowan's arm pinned behind his back. There was a clatter as the knife fell to the ground.

"Let's go," Damien instructed. His eyes still glowed faintly.

Damien and Zach began walking toward us, and we parted to let them through. Cowan twisted his head around to stare wildly at Damien. "What are you?"

Damien didn't answer. He just kept walking.

Cowan cried out again. Zach had wrenched his arm even farther behind his back. Damien put a hand on Zach's shoulder and gave him a stern look, and Zach immediately relaxed his grip on Cowan. I thought of Jared Barker, who had ganged up with his friends to nearly kill Zach when they were teenagers, all because Zach was different from the other kids at school. The only reason Zach had survived was because Damien had come to his rescue. I suspected that was one of the reasons Zach was handling Cowan so roughly. He took it personally when someone preyed on supernatural creatures.

I had assumed we would continue through the string of vignettes that led to the exit, but Damien instructed Zach to take Cowan through the same door Madge and the other witches had come through. I probably should have stayed put to entertain guests in the hospital scene, but I was too curious to know what was going to happen with

Cowan. Besides, it was nearly closing time on a Wednesday night, so there weren't a lot of people coming through, anyway.

Zach marched Cowan to the dining room. Once we got in there, Zach finally let Cowan go, pushing him roughly down onto a bench. As Zach loomed over Cowan, his back arched violently and began to contort. I remembered Gunnar had told me Zach would temporarily turn into a werewolf if he was angry or upset enough.

Without thinking, I grabbed Zach's arm and began to lead him out of the dining room. "Let's go somewhere quiet," I said in a shaking voice. I didn't even know if the transformation could stop once it had started. "Deep breaths, Zach. Deep breaths. You can control this." *I hope.*

Zach's spine began to straighten into its regular, human shape as we walked out the door into the hallway. He was doing exactly what I had instructed, taking in deep, measured breaths. Zach stopped walking as soon as we were away from the door, then he closed his eyes and leaned into me, resting his forehead on my shoulder. I rubbed his back and tried to soothe him, all while worrying my attempt to calm him would utterly fail.

Soon, though, Zach sighed and stood up straight. His voice was strained, and I knew he was still fighting the emotions that were threatening to make him change into his werewolf form. "Thank you, Olivia. I'm going outside to run off this anger. You get back in there and remember every single detail, so you can tell me later."

I promised Zach I would do just that.

CHAPTER EIGHTEEN

I didn't seem to have missed much in the dining room. Madge was going through Cowan's pockets, and as I approached, I saw her pull a glass vial filled with a purple liquid out of an inner pocket of his jacket. "Oh, Robert," Madge said in a disappointed voice. She put the vial on the table, next to an assortment of small metal charms of some sort, a wooden cross, and a compact gun.

Cowan really had arrived at the Sanctuary armed to the teeth.

"I don't think we need to ask whether you're a hunter or not," Damien said.

"I'm not looking for trouble. I only want to bring Wynn's killer to justice." Cowan had looked so defiant when we had first seen him, but he quailed under Damien's gaze.

"What about Jeff and Claw?" I asked.

Cowan flinched at those names. "I don't know what you're talking about."

I made an impatient scoffing noise. "If you're trying to protect them, it won't work. I was with them today, and they both admitted they're friends with you. Are Jeff and Claw hunters, too?"

"Claw is. Jeff retired from the life a while back," Cowan said reluctantly. "But they're not my friends."

"Is that why I saw you waving that silver knife under Jeff's nose?"

Cowan snorted out a laugh. "I knew you were keeping an eye on me, but I didn't know you were watching me that closely. I wasn't threatening Jeff. I was trying to get information about Wynn, hoping it would help me find whoever killed him. I pulled the knife out to show Jeff I was serious about taking the killer down when I found him."

"If they're not your friends, then why are you interested in finding the killer?" Damien asked. He had his arms crossed over his chest, and even though his eyes were no longer glowing, they were still boring into Cowan.

Something seemed to shift in Cowan. His tense shoulders sagged, and he dropped his head. "I didn't know Jeff had moved to this town. I was never close to him, but his hunting partner saved my life more than once. After Brandon got killed, Jeff went on a rampage, looking for the monster that had killed him. I thought it was more likely a normal human had killed him in a mugging gone bad."

"A mugging in the middle of a forest?" I asked skeptically, though I reminded myself Brandon's wallet had been emptied.

"It's as good of a theory as any," Cowan said. "Months went by, and Jeff still didn't have a lead on Brandon's killer. He gave up, saying he was done with hunting and that he was going to settle down somewhere quiet."

Madge narrowed her eyes at Cowan. "The monster hunter retired to a town with a big supernatural population. That can't be a coincidence."

Cowan raised his hands defensively. "Look, I don't know why Jeff came here. I only wound up in Nightmare because I was looking for Wynn. There have been rumors for weeks now that a hunt he and Claw had been on went sideways, and Wynn hadn't been the same since. Other hunters seemed to think he was traumatized by what had happened, but I worried it was something more. I tracked him here because I suspected he was becoming the thing he had hunted."

"A monster?" I asked.

Cowan just nodded.

"What kind of *monster*?" Madge put emphasis on the last word, clearly offended at being lumped into that category herself.

"I don't know. He was killed before I was able to find out. Possibly a ghoul or a wendigo." I saw Theo and Madge exchange a quick look at those words. "The change from human to one of those creatures takes time, and if Wynn really was going through a change, it was certainly happening slowly."

"What would you have done if you had gotten confirmation Wynn was transforming into something supernatural?" Damien asked.

"I would have done what I was trained to do." There was no emotion in Cowan's voice. He was a hunter, and he would have killed Wynn if someone hadn't gotten to him first. I realized that when I had seen Cowan in The Lusty Lunch Counter, he hadn't been staring at me, as I had thought. He had been there to spy on Wynn, observing every detail of his behavior. I wondered if Wynn had always been a creep toward women, or if his behavior toward Seraphina and Ella had been caused by this alleged transformation. I hadn't even heard of the second type of creature Cowan had mentioned, so I had no idea what symptoms Wynn might have displayed.

"I have a question," I said, actually raising my hand. "If you were willing to kill Wynn yourself, then why do you even care about finding his killer? It might have been a hunter on the same trail as you."

Cowan looked at me, his eyes straying to my ratty hospital gown, then said, "We still don't know for sure Wynn was anything other than completely human. Even if I had decided he needed to be eliminated, I would have done it mercifully, and I would have done it somewhere secluded. Killing him at the diner was sloppy and stupid."

"It made it easier to frame my friend Ella," I pointed out.

"That's the other thing. A hunter would hide the act, not frame someone else for it. His body would have never been found. Wynn's death didn't happen at the hand of a hunter, I can promise you that."

The door to the dining room banged open, and we all looked over to see Fiona stalking toward us, her face twisted in rage. Mori and Malcolm were both on her heels, and Mori was grasping at the back of Fiona's gown, like she was trying to stop her.

"How are we going to do this?" Fiona asked. "I can wail until he goes mad, unless anyone has a better suggestion."

Damien didn't raise his voice. He simply looked at Fiona and said, "No one is going to lay a hand on this man."

Fiona's chest heaved, but she didn't argue with Damien. She seemed to accept his authority, even though her nostrils flared, and she clenched her hands.

I returned my attention to Cowan and said, "You came here tonight because you assumed one of us killed Wynn." *And,* I added silently, *it could have been the banshee who's standing right here.* The way Theo was looking at Fiona told me I wasn't the only one who was thinking that.

"As soon as I got to town, I started hearing about the weird people at Nightmare Sanctuary Haunted House, and I immediately wondered if some of the people here were real monsters. That's why I asked you about the place, Olivia. I wanted to find out more, and I wanted to get a good look at you to determine whether you were something unnatural."

I bristled at being called unnatural. Seriously, how had my friends at the Sanctuary gone their whole lives being called outsiders and weirdos, and yet, somehow, they still had the capacity to be kind and generous? It was a real testament to their perseverance.

Cowan looked at Madge. "Once I found out you were working at this place, I knew my hunch was right. I hoped my presence here would pressure Wynn's killer into attacking me. I walked through the haunt slowly, and I even stopped a lot, and I made sure my hunter's weapons were visible. I wanted the killer to see me and come after me so I could take them down."

There was a lot of grumbling from everyone at the suggestion one of us had killed Wynn, but it seemed point-less to argue with Cowan. Damien leaned down until his face was just inches from Cowan's, and he said evenly, "Don't ever come back here, and don't you dare threaten any of my employees. There will be consequences. If we wanted to keep you from ever leaving, we could, but we're choosing to trust you."

Cowan swallowed hard and nodded. "If everyone here is innocent, then you have nothing to worry about. I don't want trouble."

Damien stepped back and gestured toward the door. "Then I'll escort you out."

Cowan stood right as Madge darted toward him. "Wait!" She raised a hand, her fingers bent sharply. "I will use a truth-telling spell on you, or you can just be honest. Did you ever really love me?"

I swear, Cowan's cheeks actually turned a pale shade of

pink. He looked around at all of us, then gazed at Madge sadly. "Yes."

"Did you know I was a witch when we were together in San Francisco? Were you a hunter then?"

"Yes, I was a hunter then, but I didn't know what you were. Not at first. When I finally realized you were a witch, I left town. I might be a hunter, but I'm not so ruthless that I would kill the woman I loved. Since I couldn't kill you, I knew I had to get away from you."

A tear ran down Madge's cheek, and Morgan and Maida stepped up beside her, each taking a hand. Cowan looked like he wanted to say more, but he turned and walked quickly to the door with Damien and Malcolm following.

Once the three of them had left the dining room, we all just stood there, silent. I knew we were all trying to process what had happened and everything we had learned in such a short period of time. I was still reeling from the knowledge there were actual monster hunters in the world, and I expected my friends were dealing with the news that hunters had descended on Nightmare. Maybe Jeff settling in Nightmare had been a coincidence, but I didn't get the feeling Wynn and Claw had arrived simply for a casual visit with him. There had to be more to the story.

"We were playing poker in the boiler room," Fiona said abruptly.

When we all turned to stare at her in confusion, she said, "On Friday night, when I couldn't find that awful man, I came back here. Sera and I played poker in the boiler room with Justine, Clara, and some others. So, yes, I do have an alibi."

I guess my face must have looked a lot like Theo's, and Fiona knew we had suspected her.

"You can't blame us," Theo said affably. He didn't seem at all embarrassed at being called out like that. "You came streaking into the lagoon vignette the night Wynn harassed Seraphina. You were so ready for a fight that you found out where the kid worked and went looking for him."

Fiona sounded slightly pouty as she answered, "But he wasn't there, and I didn't do anything to him."

"I believe you." Theo smiled. "Come on, let's go fill your girlfriend in on this. If we make her wait too long, she'll soak us as soon as we're within five feet of her tank."

Mori left with Theo and Fiona, and that left just me and the witches. Madge had stopped crying, but she definitely looked like someone who had just had her heart broken. It had been bad enough Cowan had up and left without a word. I imagined it was even worse to know he really had loved her, and he had abandoned her simply because she was a witch and he was a hunter. It was like some twisted, supernatural version of Romeo and Juliet.

Morgan tugged on Madge's hand, and the three witches began to move toward the door. When Madge looked up at me, I gave her a sympathetic look and whispered, "I'm so sorry." What Cowan had done wasn't my fault, but I was the one who had inadvertently reunited the two of them. If I had stayed out of the whole business of Wynn's murder, Madge might not have had her heart broken for a second time by the same man.

Of course, if I had stayed out of it, Cowan probably would have shown up at the Sanctuary, anyway.

I had never been alone in the dining room, and its high ceiling and wide expanse made me feel small and slightly lost once the witches left. Without others in the space, I could really sense its age and imagine all the patients and staff who had sat down to a meal at those tables when the place had still been a hospital.

Before I could leave, though, I needed to do something about Cowan's belongings, which were still arrayed on the table. The small medallions appeared to be occult symbols, and I expected they were meant as some kind of protective charms. The four-leaf clover was for luck, I assumed. I gingerly picked up Cowan's gun in my right hand. I was just reaching out with my left to grab the vial of purple liquid when I heard Damien say, "Don't touch it!"

CHAPTER NINETEEN

I jerked my hand back. "Why?" I asked, staring at the vial like it might rear up and bite me at any moment.

"We don't know what it is." Damien stepped up next to me. He delicately took the gun out of my hand and unloaded it in a smooth motion. He held his hand toward me so I could see the bullets resting on his palm. "Silver bullets. If Zach got shot with one of these, it would be devastating for him."

"I imagine getting shot with any kind of bullet would be devastating," I pointed out.

Damien slid the bullets into his pocket. "Yes, but it wouldn't be a matter of getting medical attention, then healing. The silver would fester inside Zach's body, weakening him."

"So silver is like poison to werewolves."

"Yes. The iron rod is, of course, to ward off ghosts and fairies. The four-leaf clover is fairy repellent as well."

So the clover isn't for luck, after all. The fairies I had met so far, including Clara, were really nice, and I had to remind myself about what Theo had told me. The supernatural creatures at the Sanctuary were the good ones, the ones Baxter had accepted into his strange extended family.

I pointed at the vial. The purple liquid inside seemed to shimmer, and even though the vial was sitting motionless on the table, the liquid inside it whirled slowly. "Madge touched the vial, and nothing bad happened to her," I noted. "Why did you tell me not to touch it?"

"Madge got lucky there wasn't anything in Cowan's pockets that could hurt a witch. I'm going to have Mori take a look at the vial. She's been around a long time, so she might have an idea what it is. In the meantime, I'm going to lock it in the office safe."

Instead of picking up the vial with his bare hands, Damien produced a handkerchief from the pocket of his black suit pants and laid it on the table. He used the butt of Cowan's gun to nudge the vial onto the handkerchief, then he gathered the four corners of the handkerchief and picked it up. Damien kept his arm extended so the vial wouldn't come close to his body. He had said he didn't know what the liquid would do, or what kind of supernatural being it would cause harm to, but I guessed he must have some idea since he was being so cautious.

I scooped up the rest of Cowan's things and followed Damien as he walked slowly to his office. We passed a few people in the hallway outside the dining room, and he told them in a sharp voice to stay back. When we reached Damien's office, he headed straight for a built-in bookcase on one wall. He pulled three books, all on different shelves and sticking a few inches out, and I heard a loud *snap*. Damien tugged on one side of the bookcase, and it swung toward him.

"The bookcase is a secret door?" I asked excitedly.

"It hides the safe." Damien glanced over his shoulder. "Shut my door, please."

By the time I had shut the door to Damien's office, he already had the safe open. He put the entire bundle, including the handkerchief, inside it delicately. "I'll take the rest of his things," he said. I plunked Cowan's charms into Damien's hand, and he placed them, the gun, and the rest of Cowan's weapons next to the vial. Then he shut the safe and swung the bookcase back into place.

"Was it like that when this place was still a hospital?" I was utterly fascinated by the idea of a hidden safe, and I had to wonder what other secrets and hidden things the old building might have.

"As far as I know. It seems a little paranoid for a hospital, doesn't it?"

"It does."

Damien turned to me. "How did you wind up in the middle of all this tonight?"

"Madge came to tell me Cowan had been spotted inside the haunt, and that he was armed. Then he walked right into the hospital vignette, where we were."

"If anyone here had seen his weapons and attacked..."

"Cowan would have fought back, and I'm guessing he would have had zero remorse for anyone he might have hurt." I shivered. If Theo had lost his temper or lunged at Cowan, the night could have gone very differently.

"You could have gotten hurt tonight, too. Not everyone can calm Zach down once he's started to turn."

I was going to reply that it was no big deal, but then I remembered the look on Zach's face when his back had started to arch. It had been terrifying, and I was surprised at myself for jumping into the middle of it. "It was a little scary," I admitted.

"It was a nice thing for you to do." Damien sat down in the desk chair, picked up a pen, then looked at me. "Well. Thanks. Have a good night."

"I'm not leaving yet." To prove my point, I sat down in one of the oxblood leather chairs in front of the desk. "We need to talk about that mine."

Damien put the pen down and laced his fingers together on top of the desk. "I told you, I don't think my father is in there."

"Maybe not, but he does own it."

Damien's eyes flashed. The light was dim compared to what I had seen earlier, and his eyes were illuminated for only a fraction of a second, but I knew I had seen it. "What?"

I nodded. "Emmett looked up the property for me. It's called Sonny's Folly Mine. Your dad bought it in the sixties."

"He never mentioned it when I was growing up."

"Why would your dad own a mine? And why in the world would he have lined it with iron to keep ghosts out?"

Damien picked up his pen again and began tapping it against the desk. "I have no idea why he would buy a mine. Maybe it was already lined with iron when he got it, and maybe it wasn't done to keep ghosts out. Iron is used for things other than warding off ghosts. Maybe the mine went bust and was turned into a vault for storing copper, and the iron was a security measure."

"Maybe. Knowing your dad owns the mine definitely brings up a lot more questions. I just wonder how many of those questions are related to his disappearance."

"I had thought him going missing was about this place." Damien stood and began to pace back and forth behind his chair. "I still think Emmett might have had something to do with Dad's disappearance, because he wanted to buy this building so desperately. Maybe it wasn't about the building, though, but that mine and whatever is inside it."

"Emmett seemed as surprised as I did when he found out who owned it."

"Then maybe somebody else is interested in the mine, and they're the ones responsible for his disappearance. Maybe you heard my father's voice because you're being drawn to the mine for some reason. It's a part of the puzzle."

"I don't know, but I'm more eager than ever to get a peek inside that mine. Can we break the lock on the door? You're Baxter's son, so I don't think you would get arrested for breaking and entering… Oh!"

Damien stopped his pacing and looked at me questioningly.

"That newspaper reporter, Ross. He told Jeff there was a warrant out for Wynn's arrest, and it's for breaking and entering. I'll bet you he and Claw were hunting something, and they got caught somewhere they weren't supposed to be. I wonder if Ross can give me more details? It might help us figure out what kind of creature Wynn was possibly turning into."

"It might. But since he's dead, I'm not sure it matters anymore."

"I guess you're right. Still, I'm frustrated that we're just getting more questions instead of answers. Every possible suspect turns out to be a dead end. Cowan admitted he would have killed Wynn if he really was transforming, and even he's seeming less likely as a suspect. There's something that we're missing, and I'm hoping that if we explore every possibility, we'll figure out what it is."

"We?" Damien laughed quietly.

"It's a team effort. By the way, there is something I would like to know that might help us figure out this mysterious mine. What is your dad? I'm guessing he ages slowly or not at all, so he has to be something supernatural."

The smile that was still playing at the corners of Damien's mouth disappeared. "How would that information help explain why he owns a mine?" he asked stiffly.

"Like I said, any information we can get is helpful. That goes for Wynn's murder as well as your dad's disappearance."

"I need to find Zach. I want to make sure he's okay. And you need to get out of that hospital getup. You look creepy." Damien walked to the door, opened it, and looked pointedly at me.

I stood and moved so I was right in front of Damien. "What is your dad?" *And why,* I wondered, *doesn't he want to tell me?*

"Good night, Olivia." Damien deftly sidestepped me and turned so he could herd me out the door. My choice was to get out or get run over by him. Once we were in the hallway, Damien stalked past me and headed toward the entryway.

"Damien, please!" I called after him. Didn't he understand I was just trying to help find Baxter?

Damien didn't stop walking, but his words drifted back to me, their tone biting. "I don't know what he is."

I made it to the entryway and stopped as I watched Damien go outside in search of Zach. Mori glided up to me. Felipe followed, his nails making loud *tick-tack* noises across the stone floor. "For once, I can't blame him for being in a mood," Mori said. "What a night."

"Yeah." I reached down to scratch Felipe's head. His gray skin was warm under my fingers. "Mori, what is Baxter?"

"No one knows."

"You said he's like a father to some of you. How can you not know what he is?"

Mori shrugged casually. "Baxter would never tell us. After a couple of decades, I finally gave up asking. He took good care of me and the others here, so ultimately, it didn't really matter what he was."

Yet another mystery, and more questions. Great.

I wished Mori a good night and walked outside. There was no sign of Zach or Damien.

When I got back to the motel, I tensed up with the fear I might run into Cowan. Thankfully, his truck wasn't in the parking lot, so he had gone somewhere else after his departure from the Sanctuary. He had probably gone to Jeff or Claw to tell them what he had experienced. I certainly hoped the incident didn't result in some kind of retaliation. No one had hurt Cowan, after all.

When I woke up on Thursday morning, I was delighted to open my door and feel a pleasant breeze. It wasn't cool outside, but it was definitely less hot. In other parts of the country, I knew it was starting to turn into fall. I wasn't sure that season really existed in Arizona, but I did, at least, appreciate the break in the heat.

I decided to take a long walk. It would let me enjoy the weather, and it would get my mind off Wynn's murder.

I hustled past Cowan's room—his truck was in its usual space, and I hoped he wasn't waiting to ambush me—and walked up to the office to say hi to Mama before I set out. I didn't even get in the door before she came rushing out of it, the newspaper clutched in her hand.

"Have you seen it? The article?" she cried.

Before I could answer, Mama thrust *The Nightmare Journal* into my hands. "On the front page, no less!"

Right there, front and center, was a photo of Ella. The headline above the article read, *The Men in Ella Griffin's Life*.

I skimmed the article. It went into detail about Ella's boyfriend, including a reference to trouble he had gotten into as a teenager for reckless driving and vandalism. There was a quote from another server at The Lusty, describing how jealous Kyle could be about Ella, and how he had once nearly started a fight with a patron who had flirted with Ella when she took his order. My eyes went to the byline, but I already knew Ross had written it. He had found his angle.

CHAPTER TWENTY

"Oh, poor Ella," I moaned. "And poor Kyle!" My eyes kept scanning the article. Ross mentioned those incidents had occurred in Albuquerque, where Kyle had grown up. That meant Ross had really gone digging for information that might cast Kyle, Ella, or anyone else related to the murder in a bad light. So much for my suggestion that Ross focus on the community rallying around Ella. I hated to think what the article might do to Kyle's reputation, and I muttered, "All for a sensational story."

Mama crossed her arms. "You need to read the last paragraph," she said ominously.

My eyes skipped to the bottom of the article, and I was shocked to see my own name in the text. Ross had concluded by mentioning other men in Ella's life were questionable, too. *Jeff Crosley, the owner of The Lusty Lunch Counter and Ms. Griffin's employer,* he had written, *was recently seen conspiring with the victim's traveling companion, who goes by the unlikely name of Claw. Nightmare newcomer Olivia Kendrick was with them for their secretive meeting at Copper Creek Campground, and sources say they were discussing the murder.*

"Are you kidding me?" I shouted at the black-and-white print. "We didn't have a secret meeting! I mean, maybe we kind of did, but it wasn't planned that way."

"I'll be writing a letter to the editor to tell him what I

think of this mudslinging," Mama said. She took the news-paper back and clutched it hard enough that it crumpled in her fist. Two guests walked into the office at that moment, and Mama's face transformed into a welcoming smile. "Good morning! Are you checking out?"

I left Mama to it and continued on my walk. Instead of heading out to get some exercise, though, I took the shortest route to the police station. I didn't even want to ask Ella any questions this time; I simply wanted to show her my support. I even stopped at the General Store on High Noon Boulevard and bought some overpriced fudge to take to her. It might not cheer Ella up, but it would, at least, taste better than jail food.

I was surprised to see several people crowded around the front desk when I walked into the police station. It had been such a sleepy place on my previous visit to Ella. I hung back, but I felt no shame in eavesdropping to find out what the people were saying.

One woman was demanding Kyle be arrested. She lifted her arm, and I saw she had the newspaper in her grip, and she started waving it in front of the officer who was sitting behind the desk.

"Now, now, I read the same article, Louise. Who among us didn't get into a little trouble during our teenage years? That's no reason to arrest the boy."

"He clearly conspired with his girlfriend!" a short, bald man said in a shaking voice.

"I suggest you all head home, and leave the police to their work. And for heaven's sake, leave the poor kid alone!"

The officer had to repeat himself a few times before the assembled people finally turned and left. They were grumbling and muttering to each other, and every single one of them eyed me with distrust on their way out.

When it was just me standing there, the officer barked,

"We are not going to arrest someone based on a silly newspaper article!"

"Good!" I agreed.

The officer opened his mouth, preparing to argue, even as he realized I was agreeing with him. "Oh. What can I help you with, then?"

"I'm just here to visit Ella."

"She sure is a popular girl. Head on back."

I didn't feel nearly as much trepidation about walking into the midst of the jail cells as I had the first time, but as soon as I saw Ella, I felt a stab of fear. She was sitting on a bench, slumped against the wall. Her hair looked tangled, and when she looked up at me, I could tell from her red eyes she had been crying.

"What happened?" I asked.

"My mom visited this morning, and she showed me that story. It's just not fair! It makes me look even more guilty. According to the newspaper, if I would date a guy with a past, then clearly, I'm not the good girl this town thought I was." Ella hiccupped and wiped at her cheeks.

"Ella, honey, that's ridiculous. The people of Nightmare know you and love you. They're not going to be swayed by the fact your boyfriend was a bit of a wild teenager." *Not counting the people who were just ranting at the front desk,* I added silently.

"My mom said the same thing. It's just that I've been in here for almost a week now, and it's a little hard to stay positive. Poor Kyle. He doesn't deserve to have his past exposed like this."

"And you don't deserve to sit in jail when you're innocent." I slid the box of fudge through the bars. "I brought you this. It's not much, but…"

Ella actually smiled as she stood to take the fudge. "It's really sweet of you. Thanks." She opened the box, grabbed a piece of fudge, and shoved it into her mouth. Once she swallowed, she said, "They've been feeding me okay, but this definitely helps me deal. Especially since yesterday was so weird."

"Weird how?"

Ella picked up another piece of fudge and waved it in my direction. "This guy came in. I'd never seen him in my life. He didn't say a word to me. He handed me a necklace that had a cross on it, and as soon as I touched it, he pulled out a bottle and squirted water on me. Then he just turned and left!"

"What did he look like?"

"A few years older than me, probably. Buzz cut. He had this big scar on his face."

"Claw."

"What?"

"The guy who came to visit you calls himself Claw. He and Wynn were traveling together, and Claw is still in town. He's staying at Copper Creek Campground."

"What a weirdo. He didn't even let me keep the necklace. He yanked it back."

"Was the cross made of metal? Iron, maybe?"

"Maybe, but I don't see what that has to do with anything."

Claw had been testing Ella to find out if she was supernatural. I wasn't sure why he would suspect her of that, unless it had something to do with Wynn's strange obsession with her. Of course, I couldn't tell Ella she had been tested with iron and what I suspected was holy water to find out if she was anything other than one hundred percent human. Instead, I said, "Maybe he wanted a little revenge for what happened to Wynn. It was mean of him to do that to you."

"Yeah. Jerk."

I chatted with Ella for a while longer, then left when Kyle arrived to see her. I figured the two of them were about to have a long conversation regarding that newspaper article. I walked home, and I was so absorbed in my thoughts that I made it all the way to the back of the motel before I realized there was a police car at the foot of the stairs leading up to my apartment. I slowed down and came to a stop a short distance away as two officers climbed out of the car.

"Olivia Kendrick?" one of them asked.

"That's her," the other confirmed.

"Hi, Officer Reyes," I said. "What's going on?"

"Where were you at four o'clock this morning?"

It was only then I noticed how intently Officer Reyes was looking at me. "I was in bed, asleep," I said. My limbs felt cold. "Why?"

"Because you're the prime suspect in an assault. Someone at Copper Creek Campground says you broke into his van at four a.m. and assaulted him."

"Someone attacked Claw?"

"You know the victim, then." The other officer crossed his arms and smirked, as if I had just admitted guilt.

I ignored him and focused my attention on Officer Reyes. "Is Claw okay?"

"He's a little banged up. Luckily, he was able to beat off his attacker with a cast-iron pan."

Iron! I gasped. Had Claw used the pan because it was the closest thing he could grab, or had his attacker been supernatural? Cowan had shown up at the Sanctuary because he suspected someone there had killed Wynn, and Claw had performed tests on Ella to find out if she was supernatural. That meant both of them suspected Wynn's killer wasn't human.

The officer I was trying so hard to ignore stepped toward me. "We're taking you in."

I raised my hands and fought the urge to turn and run. "But why am I a suspect?"

Officer Reyes gave me a look that almost seemed sympathetic. "Because the victim recognized his attacker, and he said it was you."

"That is utterly ridiculous," I said, even as the other officer continued moving toward me. He was close enough that I could see his name badge. Officer Wilkins.

"It is ridiculous," said a voice to my right.

I looked over to see Cowan, who was standing in the doorway of his motel room. He was leaning against the doorframe with his arms crossed, and he looked like he was enjoying the scene.

"Stay out of this," Officer Reyes warned.

Cowan didn't heed the advice. "I had insomnia last night, so I came out for some fresh air. Her car was in the parking lot, and I didn't see her coming or going." He pointed at the stairs. "That's the only way in or out of her place."

I seriously doubted Cowan was telling the truth, and I had no idea why he would vouch for me, especially if he had to lie to do it. After everything that had happened with him at the Sanctuary, it made zero sense.

Officer Wilkins didn't seem to think it made any sense, either. "The victim identified Ms. Kendrick as his assailant," he said crisply.

"Then I think we should all sit down and talk to him. Clearly, he's mistaken."

"If you want to go to the police station, too, you're more than welcome." Officer Wilkins turned away from me and opened the rear door of the police car. "We've got room for one more."

Before I knew it, I was sitting in the back of a police car next to Cowan. I wanted to ask him what was going on, but there was no way to do it without being overheard. I tried to give him a look that conveyed my confusion, but

Cowan just gazed out the window and remained silent on the entire drive.

It was ironic that I had just been at the police station, and I was suddenly there again. It was almost a shame the two officers had to waste a trip to the motel to fetch me, when they could have just steered me into an office after my visit with Ella.

Cowan and I were taken into a cramped conference room. The chairs were plastic and not very comfortable, and the table was cluttered with stacks of manilla folders and paperwork. Once Cowan and I were seated next to Officer Wilkins, Officer Reyes left and came back a few minutes later with Claw.

Claw had a big bruise on his forehead, and he limped slightly. When he saw me, he actually looked scared. He sat down at the table, picking a chair that was as far away from me as possible. It was only then that he seemed to realize Cowan was sitting next to me. Claw raised his eyebrows questioningly at Cowan, but he was gazing at the far wall and didn't even acknowledge Claw's presence.

Officer Reyes pointed at me. "Is this the person who attacked you?" he asked Claw.

I wanted to jump up and shout that it hadn't been me, but I stayed still while Claw looked at me fearfully. "Yes, it was her. Olivia tried to kill me."

CHAPTER TWENTY-ONE

As soon as Claw said that, I did jump up and shout, "No, I didn't!" Claw shrank against the back of his chair, and he reached a hand up to clutch at his shirt.

No, I realized. *Not his shirt. The iron cross under his shirt. The one he got Ella to touch.* Even though I was human, Claw's hunter instincts had him grabbing for something that could repel me.

"Ms. Kendrick, please sit down," Officer Wilkins said.

I sat, but I didn't stop defending myself. "I was in bed, asleep, when Claw was attacked. Why would I go after him, anyway?"

"That's one of the things we're going to find out." Wilkins plunked a tape recorder down in the middle of the table. "Let's chat. Mr. Fairbanks isn't even a Nightmare resident, but when we mentioned the assault happened at the campground, you immediately knew who we were referring to."

"Claw is the only person I know at the campground," I said sullenly.

"How do you know Mr. Fairbanks, anyway?" Wilkins continued.

I think this is the point where I'm supposed to refuse to say anything until I have a lawyer. That thought made my heart race. Was I really in danger of being charged with assault?

As far as I knew, Claw had nothing against me, so why was he falsely accusing me of attacking him? I was trying to help find his friend's killer, and there he was, telling the police I was a violent criminal.

I was so upset and confused that I didn't say anything. I just sat there, stunned. I was staring at Claw, but I wasn't really seeing him. Instead, I was seeing a rapid-fire slideshow of everything that had happened in the past week. Wynn's death, Ella caught on video even though she swore she had been sleeping at the time, Cowan's strange appearance in Nightmare, Jeff's past as a hunter and his relationship to Wynn, and finally, me being accused of assault even though I...

"Oh!" I exclaimed.

Wilkins looked at me keenly.

Even though I had been sleeping at the time.

Claw wasn't falsely accusing me. He really believed I had attacked him. I had been framed, just like Ella. Both of us had been sound asleep while someone went on the attack, making it look like each of us was guilty. And, I suspected, the same person had been behind both Wynn's murder and the attack on Claw. If we could find out who had framed me, then we would know who had killed Wynn, too.

"Would you care to elaborate on that, Ms. Kendrick?" Officer Reyes, unlike his partner, still spoke and acted like he thought I might be innocent.

I blinked at Officer Reyes. My mind was already making a list of tasks that might help us get answers—like asking Claw if he saw what his attacker had been driving and questioning other campers to find out if they had witnessed anything—and it took me a moment to steer my thoughts back to the conversation happening around me.

I glanced at Cowan, and he shook his head almost

imperceptibly before he turned to Claw. "I like your necklace," Cowan told him.

Claw's fingers were still wrapped around the necklace under his shirt. He tilted his head and narrowed his eyes, clearly trying to understand why Cowan had just said that. "Thanks," Claw mumbled.

Cowan reached his arm across the table. "May I see it, please?"

I was watching Cowan closely, and I saw the way his head turned, ever so slightly, in my direction. Claw's eyes widened, and he looked from Cowan to me several times. Without a word, he reached back and unclasped his necklace. He pulled the black cord out from under his collar, and I saw that the cross was about two inches long. It danced on the cord as Claw handed it over.

Cowan put the cross in his palm, nodded, then handed it to me. "Isn't it lovely?" he asked.

My fingers curled around the cross as I realized what Cowan was doing. He was proving to Claw that I wasn't something that was affected by iron. I wasn't a ghost—I mean, that was obvious—a fairy, or whatever kind of creature iron could repel or harm.

It was that "whatever" part that especially interested me. My eye color and the shape of my ears would have given me away if I were a fairy, so that meant there was some kind of supernatural creature that looked completely human but was vulnerable to iron.

I made a point of looking right at Claw so he could see I wasn't affected at all by the cross. It wasn't burning my palm or making me cry out or any of the things I expected it would do if I was vulnerable to it.

"It looked just like you," Claw said.

"But it wasn't me. Someone framed me the same way they framed Ella."

"The same person framed both women," Cowan said.

He spoke slowly, enunciating each word clearly, and I knew he was trying to convey something to Claw that he didn't want to say in front of the police. I had already figured out Ella and I had been framed by the same person, so I wasn't sure why Cowan didn't want to say it outright.

"What are you talking about?" Officer Wilkins broke in. "Ms. Griffin wasn't framed. We have surveillance video that puts her at the scene of the murder."

Claw ignored Wilkins. Instead, he looked at Officer Reyes while pointing at me. "I was mistaken. This isn't the person who attacked me."

Reyes looked incredulous. "You just identified her as your attacker five minutes ago."

"And, as I said, I was mistaken. It was dark inside my van when I was attacked. I could just see the auburn hair, and I assumed it was Olivia. Now that I'm sitting right across from her in a bright room, though, I realize she isn't who I saw in my van."

Words came out of Reyes's mouth, but he wasn't able to complete a full sentence. "But... You can't possibly... This has got to be..."

Claw smacked his palms against the table and stood. "I guess the Nightmare Police Department will have to continue looking for my attacker, because it definitely wasn't Olivia. Gentlemen, thank you for your time and continued efforts on my behalf." Claw looked at me, and in a tone that sounded sincere, he said, "Olivia, I am so sorry I accused you of attacking me. I know it wasn't you, and I apologize for the embarrassment and inconvenience this must have caused."

I wasn't even sure how to respond to that. I was so surprised by the sudden turn of events that I was in a slight daze, though something resembling words came out of my mouth. I didn't even get up as everyone else began to move out of the room. Cowan had to take me gently by the arm and prod me into standing.

"We'll keep looking for some other auburn-haired woman," Wilkins said as I followed Cowan and Claw out the front door of the police station. He didn't bother to hide his sarcasm, and he was eyeing Claw like he had become the suspect rather than the victim.

I was still in a daze when we were outside and standing on the sidewalk. Cowan and Claw were talking rapidly and quietly to each other, their heads close. Suddenly, Cowan looked at me. "Can we go to your place? We need to talk somewhere we won't be watched or overheard."

"Sure." I realized I was still clutching Claw's necklace, and I handed it back to him. "I'm not supernatural," I told him, "but I am curious to know what iron repels other than ghosts and fairies."

"Not here," Cowan said crisply. "Do you want the police to overhear you talking like that?"

He had a point. The three of us barely spoke during the walk back to Cowboy's Corral, even though I was dying to ask about a hundred questions.

It was strange ushering Cowan and Claw into my apartment, especially since Cowan had been on my suspect list from the start. As soon as I shut the door, Claw said, "You're right, Rhodes, the police won't find the person who killed Wynn and attacked me." It was like he was continuing a conversation I somehow hadn't heard.

"Why not?" I asked. "I think it's safe to assume one person is responsible for both incidents, but I don't understand why you think they'll get away with it."

"They won't get away with it," Claw said. "We'll make sure of that."

"You think the police won't be able to find the person, but you will?" I couldn't imagine what resources Claw had that the police didn't.

Claw hesitated, then looked at Cowan.

"She knows," Cowan said. "About the shadow world and what you and I do for a living."

"How?" Claw waved his hands. "Never mind. That's a discussion for another time." He gave me a look that said he still didn't entirely trust me.

"She even works with supernatural creatures," Cowan prompted.

"This is a whole different thing, though." Claw took a deep breath, then returned his attention to me. "The reason the police won't catch the person who attacked me is because it was you who attacked me."

"First of all," I said, "I didn't attack you. And second, you just sat there and told the police it wasn't me, so why are you back to thinking I did it?"

Claw smirked at me. "You might have solved one murder in this town, but this is unlike any situation you or the police have ever seen. When I say you attacked me, I mean it: it was your face, your hair, even your voice. And when Ella supposedly killed Wynn, it looked exactly like her on that security video."

"So, what, Ella and I both have murderous doppelgängers running around Nightmare? I've seen the video of Ella, and it's definitely her. No one can disguise themselves that well."

Claw shook his head and looked at me grimly. "A shapeshifter can."

CHAPTER TWENTY-TWO

"That's not fair!" I said loudly. And, if I'm being honest, maybe I had a bit of a hysterical edge to my voice, too.

"No, it's not," Cowan agreed. "It makes it much more difficult to catch a killer when they can shift to look like anyone else."

"But you can use iron to identify them," I said.

Claw nodded. "We didn't know we were dealing with a shapeshifter. Cowan and I both suspected Wynn was killed by a monster, but shapeshifters are incredibly rare. When I grabbed the cast-iron pan to fight off my attacker—to fight you off, as I thought—I was surprised at how quickly they retreated. I figured it was because I was harder to subdue than they had expected. Now I realize it was the iron doing the fighting, not me."

I frowned. "If a shapeshifter is living in Nightmare, then surely my friends at the Sanctuary would know about it."

"How?" Cowan walked to the window next to the kitchenette and peered out. "They look like a normal human, unless they choose to take on a monster form."

I had been standing, but that statement made me sit down heavily on the foot of my bed. "So the shapeshifter really could be someone at the Sanctuary." I said it softly, more to myself than anything. It was a terrifying thought.

"They could be." Cowan sat down next to me. "I went to the haunted house looking for Wynn's murderer, but it hadn't yet occurred to me that it could be a shapeshifter. I had thought someone had doctored the security video, maybe taking old footage of Ella and adding the time-stamp to make it look like she had been in the diner the night Wynn was killed. I wasn't thinking like a hunter. Then, when the police arrived and said you had attacked Wynn, it finally clicked."

"I appreciate you standing up for me today," I said sincerely. "After everything that happened at the Sanctuary, you had no reason to be nice, but you were."

"I had every reason to be nice: you and your co-workers let me go."

"That's because my co-workers are supernatural, but they're not monsters." Cowan's mouth twitched when I said that, and I knew he was thinking of Madge's reaction to being called a monster. Not wanting to dive back into that subject, I said, "What do we do now? Should we put iron all over town? Do we go door to door and throw holy water on everyone, like Claw did to Ella?"

Claw chuckled. "That was water from a pond in Salem. It's used to detect a witch. Holy water doesn't actually do anything, despite what you see in vampire movies."

I leaned forward and rested my elbows on my knees. "You tested Ella with iron and some kind of witch water. Why did you think she might be supernatural?"

"Wynn was kind of obsessed with her. He'd come back to the campground and go on and on about her. I thought maybe she was putting him under some kind of spell or thrall. I also suspected Ella wasn't doing anything at all, and the obsession had more to do with Wynn's trans-formation."

I exchanged a look with Cowan. "So he *was* turning into something supernatural," I said.

"Yeah. He was bitten by a ghoul at an abandoned factory outside Albuquerque. Ghouls can become obsessed with a living person, like Wynn did with Ella." Claw ran a hand over his clipped hair. "Sorry I lied about it, Rhodes. I was afraid you'd kill me, just in case I'd been bitten, too."

"Do you think Wynn was killed because he was transforming?" I didn't know what a ghoul was, exactly, but it didn't sound good. I returned to my earlier thought that another hunter could have gone after Wynn.

Cowan shook his head. "I stand by what I said. This wasn't the work of a hunter."

"Agreed," Claw said.

So much for that theory, I thought. "Do either of you have experience with shapeshifters?" When both men shook their heads, I continued. "Maybe someone at the Sanctuary does. Even if you still think the shapeshifter is there, I know there are some trustworthy people we can talk to about this. However, I don't think either one of you is exactly welcome there. I can talk to my friends tonight, then let you know what they say."

"I think that's safest," Cowan said. "But please leave Madge out of this. I don't want to put her in danger."

I nodded. "I can do that."

There wasn't a lot to say after that, so Cowan and Claw left shortly after. They both wanted to review all their research about shapeshifters to give them the best advantage possible. As for me, I just wanted to lie down on my bed and try to process everything that had happened.

It had only been a couple of weeks since I had learned that supernatural creatures even existed, and here I was being told shapeshifters were a real thing, and they could literally get away with murder because they could look like anyone they wanted to. Not only that, but a shapeshifter had decided to disguise itself as me. Clearly, I was poking my nose into Wynn's murder a little too publicly.

Either that, or someone I knew was a shapeshifter. Nope, I wasn't going to go there. I trusted my friends.

I could only stand to be alone with my whirling mind for so long. Eventually, I got up and went to the front office. I could hear Mama talking on the phone behind the front desk, and when she stood to see who had come in the door, she pointed at me, then at one of the chairs in the lobby. I sat dutifully.

After she wrapped up her call, Mama came around the desk to stand in front of me with her hands on her hips. "What were the police doing here? And why did you and Cowan Rhodes get hauled to the police station? I didn't see any handcuffs, so I'm hoping you're not in trouble."

"Wynn's friend Claw, the one he came to Nightmare with, got attacked in his camper last night," I said. "In the dark, Claw thought it was me. Cowan knows Claw, so he went to the police station along with me to talk it out. Claw realized he had misidentified his attacker, and we all left."

"What kind of mother names her kid Claw?"

I laughed. "That's your takeaway from the story?"

Mama sighed and sat down next to me. "I assume Claw was attacked by the same person who killed Wynn and framed Ella for it."

"That's our guess."

"And if Cowan is friends with Claw, then he's probably not our murderer."

"Probably not. But"—I held up a warning finger—"I think we should continue keeping an eye on him. After all, he did give you the heebie jeebies." I didn't add that Mama's feeling had been completely justified, considering Cowan was a monster hunter who carried a long knife around.

Mama promised to stay vigilant before adding, "You be careful, and don't hesitate to ask Damien to stay with you if you think you need the protection."

"I would have to be in a lot of danger for that to happen." I was able to steer the conversation away from Cowan then, and by the time I headed back to my apartment to get ready for work, my mind felt a little more at ease. Hanging out with Mama had reminded me there were nice, normal, non-murderous things to appreciate about Nightmare.

I left for work early that evening because I wanted to start asking around about shapeshifters. When I arrived, the ticket window was open, and I looked through it to see Zach sitting at a desk in the cramped room, going through some paperwork. "Hey," I called.

"Hi," Zach grumbled. He and I were friends, but that didn't change the fact he was usually grumpy when he wasn't in werewolf form.

"You got a minute?"

Zach didn't even look up from his work. "No. Damien asked me to rerun the numbers from last weekend. He seems to think I did it wrong the first time."

I made a noise of disgust, and Zach nodded his head in agreement while he continued poring over the papers. As the Sanctuary's accountant, he was under a lot of pressure from Damien, so I said, "We'll talk later, then. I just wanted to know what you could tell me about shapeshifters."

That got Zach's full attention. He dropped his pen and whipped around to look at me. "Why do you want to know about them?"

"Because someone who looked exactly like me attacked Wynn's friend Claw. We're assuming it was the same shapeshifter who framed Ella for Wynn's murder."

"Ohhh." Zach stood up and came to the window. He leaned toward me and curled his fingers around the edge of the small countertop that was fitted to the window frame. "That makes sense. How did we not think of it already?"

"Apparently, shapeshifters are rare, so who would have thought one was in Nightmare?"

"They're extremely rare," Zach said thoughtfully. "I think it's likely those guys were followed here."

"Have there ever been shapeshifters at the Sanctuary?"

"Not that I know of. Baxter would know, of course, but we can't exactly ask him."

I could hear the strain in Zach's voice, and I put my hand over one of his. It was so easy to focus on everyone's dislike of Damien that I sometimes forgot how much my friends were grieving Baxter's disappearance. Zach gave me a small smile and made me promise to keep him filled in, then I went in search of the others.

Mori and Theo were in the hallway that led to the dining room, so I hailed them, and they turned, looking surprised to see me so early. I told them about the attack on Claw, and they both recoiled when I said we suspected it was a shapeshifter.

"Oh, not another one," Theo said disdainfully.

"Another one? There's been one in Nightmare before?" I asked. I noticed even Mori seemed surprised by Theo's statement.

"No, I met one about two hundred years ago. I had to deliver a chest of gold coins to a rival pirate. It's a long story, but basically, we paid him rent so we could sail in what he called 'his' waters. Anyway, I delivered the chest to him, and that was that, until three months later, when his ship attacked ours. He claimed we had never paid up. As it turned out, I had given the gold to a shapeshifter who had taken on the form of the pirate to steal our treasure."

The story sounded like something from a book of fairy tales, and I suppressed a laugh. "Did you make him walk the plank when you found out?"

"Worse." Theo grinned at me. "But we're still getting to know each other, and I don't want to scare you off."

Yikes.

"I've never met a shapeshifter," Mori said, "but I do know they die in the same ways humans do. Old age, disease, illness. You don't have to do anything special like you do with, say, vampires."

"They look like humans, and they die like humans," I said. "It seems like iron is the only way to detect one."

"Or you catch them in the midst of a change. I would imagine that's a dead giveaway." Mori wrinkled her nose. "Ew."

"You said the shapeshifter impersonated you to attack this Claw guy," Theo said.

"Yeah. I'm afraid looking into Wynn's murder has put me in danger."

"Maybe, but I think Claw is the one who's really in danger. That shifter went after him, not you."

"He's the next target," I agreed. "Fake Me didn't go to that van just to scare him."

Mori nodded. "That means Claw is the best chance we have for drawing the shapeshifter out of hiding."

"Are you suggesting we set a trap and use Claw as bait?" I asked. It seemed cruel and scary and, I realized, exactly like something a hunter might do. Claw would probably agree to it in a heartbeat if it led to finding Wynn's killer.

Mori and Theo both looked uncomfortable with the idea, but Mori said, "If he's willing, it might be our best bet. I originally wanted to help find the killer just so your friend wouldn't take the blame, Olivia. Now, it's a lot more than that. Nightmare doesn't need a rogue shapeshifter roaming around."

It surprised me how uncomfortable Mori, Theo, and even Zach seemed to be when it came to shapeshifters. I hadn't stopped to consider that one type of supernatural creature might be afraid of another. I took a deep breath and sat up straight. "Let's come up with a plan."

CHAPTER TWENTY-THREE

The dining room filled up as everyone arrived for that night's family meeting, and we were still debating how to draw the shapeshifter out of hiding. By the time Justine stepped up to the podium to address us, we had been joined by Zach, Malcolm, and even Damien. I wasn't sure what had brought him into the dining room to begin with, but he came right over to our table, looked at me, and said, "What kind of trouble are you in now?"

"Good evening!" Justine called from the podium. She was glaring at Damien, and although he glared right back, he quietly squeezed his way onto the bench between Theo and me. Justine assigned me to the front door, as usual, and after that I stopped listening to her. I had come up with a plan that was probably ridiculous and might get shot down, but I was ready to present it after the meeting wrapped up.

No sooner had Justine set us loose than Damien said, "What have you gotten yourself into, Olivia?"

"I haven't done anything," I said defensively.

"That's not what they're saying in town."

Oh, no. Despite Claw retracting his accusation, gossip about me attacking someone was apparently still spreading through town. I put my head in my hands. "I didn't attack anyone. I was in bed, asleep, when it happened."

I heard Mori say, "It was a shapeshifter."

Damien was sitting close enough to me that I felt the way he stiffened. "A shapeshifter? Here in Nightmare?"

"They impersonated Ella when they killed Wynn, and they impersonated me when they tried to kill Claw at four o'clock this morning," I said, raising my head. "We've been trying to figure out how we can catch them, and I think I have a plan."

"Let's hear it, then." Malcolm said.

"This is going to sound silly," I warned. I was already second-guessing my crazy idea. "The shapeshifter will know not to break into Claw's van again. Maybe they couldn't sense the iron in there the way Tanner and McCrory could, but they know now that it's in there, and that Claw can use even a cast-iron pan as an effective weapon. What we need to do, then, is get Claw out into the open somewhere, where he will seem vulnerable."

"That doesn't sound silly to me," Theo said.

"Because I haven't gotten to the silly part yet. I've been going to a lot of yard sales lately, and I think that's how we can tempt the shapeshifter into the open. Claw can put the word out that he's having a yard sale. It makes sense he might want to sell off some of Wynn's things. He can even have it at a strange time, like six to midnight, so the shapeshifter can attack in the darkness."

"You think if Claw is standing in the middle of an open space, the killer might try again?" Malcolm looked doubtful.

"I think it's a decent idea," Mori said. "Like you just said, Olivia, it gets Claw out into the open. And for a guy who doesn't have a job, it makes sense he would want to get some extra cash. There isn't anything suspicious about that setup."

I looked at Malcolm, one eyebrow raised.

"I think it's worth a shot," he said. He had taken off his

top hat, and he turned it slowly in his long, thin hands. "If nothing else, Claw makes a few bucks."

"I'll go by the campground after work to run the idea past him. I expect he's the nocturnal type. Tomorrow, he can put up flyers or place a notice in the paper, then he can have the sale on Saturday."

Damien cleared his throat, and I sighed inwardly. I should have known he would have something against my plan.

"Please, Damien, tell me how stupid my plan is and why we shouldn't do it." The snark just fell out of my mouth, and I immediately felt bad. I kept failing on my promise to Mama to go easy on Damien, but he just made it so hard to do. He seemed impossible to placate.

So it was a big surprise when Damien said, "I don't think it's a stupid plan at all."

Still, I knew there was a *but* coming.

"But…"

Yup, there it is.

"I'm going with you to the campground tonight. If the killer impersonated you for the attack, that means you're on their radar, and you could be in just as much danger as Claw."

I had to admit, Damien made a good point. I agreed to let him go with me, and our planning session broke up shortly after that. Theo still had to put on his zombie makeup, and Mori said something about having a quick snack before the haunt opened at eight o'clock. I wondered how much blood qualified as a snack for her.

Work that night absolutely dragged. I was anxious to set our plan into motion so we could find the shapeshifter, get them to confess to the murder, and clear Ella's name. When it was time for my break, I munched on my usual chips and cookies in the dining room, but I never sat down. Instead, I paced back and forth between a row of tables. Mori complained just watching me was wearing her out, but Felipe seemed to enjoy it. He trotted alongside me and gobbled up any crumbs that fell from my fingers.

The final guests of the night walked past me at fifteen minutes before midnight. I started pacing again, moving between the front door and the ticket window, until Zach told me to please settle down. In response, I confined myself to pacing a tight circle in front of the door until we got word the last guests had exited the building, and we were done for the night.

I practically flew down the hall to the locker room to grab my purse, but I forced myself to slow my pace as I walked to Damien's office. I didn't want him to see how tightly wound I was. If I was making Mori and Zach uncomfortable, then it would probably bother Damien, too, and I was in no mood for a lecture from him.

"Hey," I said as I walked into his office. "I'm ready when—oh." I stopped walking and averted my eyes. Damien was standing behind his desk, shirtless. His button-down shirt and suit coat were draped across the desk, and he was just picking up a black T-shirt as I walked in. I also noticed he was wearing blue jeans, and I was grateful I hadn't walked in while he had been changing into those.

"Really?" Damien sounded like he was trying to keep himself from laughing. "Are you that modest?"

"No." I looked up to prove I wasn't a prude, but Damien already had the T-shirt on. I had never seen him dressed so casually. He looked handsome in a suit, but his muscles were hidden under all the material. In jeans and a T-shirt, I could appreciate his physique.

He had looked even better without a shirt at all. It really irked me that such a jerk was so attractive. It just didn't seem fair.

Damien was staring at me, a small smile on his face.

"I was just surprised, that's all," I said quickly. "I didn't know this was a changing room as well as an office."

Damien gestured at himself. "I figured my suit would stand out too much at the campground. Let's go."

On our way to the grassy parking lot next to the building, Damien offered to drive. I emphatically told him no. If showing up at Copper Creek Campground in a suit was too conspicuous, then surely showing up in a silver Corvette was, too.

Seeing Damien shirtless had calmed my nerves for a few minutes. I was so busy thinking about how good he had looked that I didn't have space in my brain to fret about the plan. As I drove toward the campground, though, I could feel my nervousness returning, and I tapped the steering wheel with my index fingers. Damien looked at me but remained silent.

I didn't bother to hide the car down a side road this time. I found a place to park that wasn't too far from Claw's van, and as Damien and I got closer to the campsite, I could see Claw sitting in a folding chair. It was positioned between the side of his van and a roaring campfire.

Claw stood when he spotted us. His hands were gripping the alleged fire poker I had seen in the van before, and I realized it had to be some kind of spear for fighting supernatural creatures. A hunter's weapon. Claw expected to be attacked again.

"It's me, Olivia," I called. To make sure he knew it was truly me, and not the imposter who had attacked him, I said, "Really, actually Olivia. I held your necklace at the police station this morning. And this is Damien Shackleford. He runs Nightmare Sanctuary."

In answer, Claw reached out with the blunt end of the spear facing us. I curled my fingers around it, then instructed Damien to do the same. Once we had both proven we could touch iron without any ill effects, Claw relaxed and held the spear loosely at his side. "What brings you out here?"

I laid out my plan for the yard sale, and Claw smiled when I finished. "You don't think like a hunter, which is an advantage here. I doubt I could have come up with such an innocent-sounding plan. Well done. I just have one request: will you accompany me tomorrow? I'll design a flyer on my laptop, but I don't want to wander around town by myself. I would ask Cowan, but I think involving him might seem too obvious if the shapeshifter is watching."

Damien grumbled about that request, but I agreed to it. I told Claw I would meet him at eleven o'clock the following morning at the coffee shop on High Noon Boulevard, then wished him a good night. I expected he wouldn't be sleeping at all, and I nearly invited him to stay with me so he wouldn't be alone in the middle of the campground. But, I told myself, if he didn't feel safe alone, he could have asked to stay with Cowan. Plus, no matter how bad I felt for Claw, I still wasn't quite sure I could trust him.

As we drove back to the Sanctuary, I could practically feel the tension coming from Damien.

"What?" I prompted.

"I don't like it. You being the bodyguard for a hunter who's been targeted by a shapeshifter. I think I should join you tomorrow, too."

"We'll be out in broad daylight, Damien. What do you really think is going to happen?"

"Bad things don't just happen at night," Damien said ominously. "Remember, you found Jared Barker's body before the sun went down."

"Wynn was killed at night, and Claw was attacked at night. I don't think the shapeshifter is a big fan of committing crime in the daylight."

Damien ignored my admittedly terrible logic. Of

course it was dangerous for me to go with Claw, but I was the one asking him to put his neck on the line so we could catch Wynn's killer. It was only fair that I should do everything in my power to keep him as safe as possible.

"Do you still have that cell phone?" Damien asked.

"No, that was Lucy's. Mama's granddaughter. Lucy had left it at the motel, so Mama loaned it to me that one time."

"It saved your life that day."

"I know."

Damien didn't say anything else to me until we got back to the Sanctuary. I pulled up behind his car and stopped. "Thanks for your help tonight. I'll see you tomorrow," I said.

"We're not done just yet," Damien said as he opened the passenger-side door. "Come on."

I turned off the ignition and got out of my car warily. Damien was already walking toward the entrance to the building, so I followed. The front doors were locked, but he produced a key and went inside, then headed for his office.

Damien told me to shut the office door once we were inside, and I wondered if he was about to open the secret safe again. Instead, though, he sat down at his desk and opened a drawer. He pulled a cell phone out of it and handed it to me, along with a charging cord. "This is my father's. I've been keeping it charged in case someone calls who might have information about him. You can use it until he comes back."

Damien's voice broke on that last word. There was no reason for him to articulate what I knew we were both thinking: *if he comes back.*

Having Lucy's phone on me at Barker Ranch really had saved my life, so I accepted Baxter's phone gratefully. There was a certain irony that I had found the job at Nightmare Sanctuary through a notice written in Baxter's hand, I had recently heard his voice coming from Sonny's Folly Mine, and now I was going to start using his cell phone as my own.

Maybe Damien is right. There really is a connection between Baxter and me. I still didn't think it made me a conjuror or any kind of supernatural creature, but it was all beginning to feel like more than a coincidence.

As I was tucking the phone and charger into my purse, I noticed Damien walking toward me out of the corner of my eye. I looked up to see he had a fine silver chain in his hands. There were two charms dangling from it. One was a tiny cross and the other was a pentagram.

"Was this your dad's, too?"

"It was my mother's," Damien said quietly. He stepped behind me and brought the chain down in front of my face. I instinctively reached back and pulled my hair away from the nape of my neck. As Damien clasped the necklace, he said, "My father had a witch put a protection spell on it, and I think you need all the help you can get. Anyone you meet could be the shapeshifter. Don't trust anyone, Olivia. Not Claw, not Cowan. Not even me."

CHAPTER TWENTY-FOUR

I arrived early at the coffee shop on Friday morning. Damien's warning had spooked me, and I didn't want to be in a rush, which might make me overlook any signs that something was amiss. The Caffeinated Cadaver was housed in what had once been Nightmare's mortuary, and it sat on top of the supernatural bar Under the Undertaker's. I ordered a latte and sat down at a small table in the far corner. My chair was against the wall, so I could see anyone approaching. I really didn't need the caffeine; I was already on high alert.

Claw must have been feeling a bit jittery himself. He arrived exactly at eleven o'clock, but he stopped a few feet away from me and said, "I told you it was just a fire poker."

"And my apartment has an orange shag rug," I answered. "You sat on the loveseat, next to Cowan."

Claw seemed satisfied I really was myself, so he sat down opposite me. "I started going through some of Wynn's stuff, and we really can make this look like a legit yard sale. He had a surprising amount of junk crammed into our van."

"Good." I hesitated for a moment, then said, "You know, I never really expressed my condolences. First, I

165

thought you were a suspect. Then, I got so wrapped up in trying to help Ella that I forgot about the fact you had just lost a friend. I know this must be hard for you."

"A hunter's life is dangerous. I've lost people before, but no one so close. It hurts, but I'm as determined as you are to find this shifter. Catching Wynn's killer is going to make me feel a whole lot better."

"I'm sure it will. Where do you want to start today?"

Claw patted the beat-up leather messenger bag he'd brought with him. "I designed the flyers, so I need to find a printer and a copy machine somewhere. I figure I should put a notice in the classifieds, too. Whatever helps get the word out increases our chances of getting the shifter's attention."

Claw pulled his laptop out of the bag, then he opened it up and showed me the flyer design. It was simple, but it was right in line with the plan we had come up with at the Sanctuary: he would set up in the Copper Creek Campground parking lot on Saturday afternoon. He had changed the hours to three o'clock until nine, saying that sounded more plausible than going until midnight.

"We can keep watch, you know," I told him. "Some of us from the Sanctuary can hide ourselves nearby. If there's any trouble, we'll be by your side in an instant."

"I would appreciate that."

I sat back in my chair and thought about what I had just said. Just when I thought my life in Nightmare couldn't get any more bizarre, it did. I was offering supernatural protection to a monster hunter who was trying to draw out a murderous shapeshifter.

Seriously, who am I? Nashville Olivia wouldn't recognize Nightmare Olivia.

I took a last swig of my latte, then asked the man behind the counter to point us in the direction of a printer.

Soon, Claw and I were walking along High Noon Boulevard toward the library, where I had been told we would find several old but still operable printers.

The Nightmare public library was about a five-minute walk from The Caffeinated Cadaver. It was in a squat wooden building just off High Noon Boulevard, and a historic plaque in front of it said the building was originally the town's newspaper office. Which, the sign informed me, had moved to the building across the street back in the eighteen nineties. I turned around and, sure enough, there was a two-story building with a sign that read *The Nightmare Journal* in a Wild West–style font.

"I think it will be safe for us to divide and conquer on this one," Claw said, turning to see what I was looking at. "I doubt I'll be in danger at the library."

"Okay. I'll go place the ad, and as soon as you're done making copies, come inside the newspaper office and find me." I glanced up and down the street. Plenty of tourists were walking on the sidewalks, on their way to the touristy shops and restaurants along High Noon Boulevard. It would be so easy for a shapeshifter to blend right in. "Try not to be outside on your own too much."

"I'll see you soon."

Claw went into the library, and I turned and waited for a string of cars to go past before I could cross the street. It was only Friday, but the weekend seemed to have started early for tourist traffic.

When I opened the front door to the newspaper office, I was hit with a musty smell. I imagined there was a room somewhere in the building that housed every issue *The Nightmare Journal* had ever published, right back to the eighteen hundreds.

There was a reception desk in front of me. Behind that, there was open space, with desks squeezed in as tightly as possible. Only about half of them were currently occupied, and I wondered if Nightmare had been so big during its mining heyday that it really had needed that many spots for journalists to cover the news. Sunlight streamed through the windows, and the room buzzed quietly from phone conversations and chatter among the journalists.

I stepped up to the reception desk, where a man wearing a crisp white button-down shirt sat. "Hi, there," I said. "I'd like to place a classified notice for a yard sale. Where can I do that?"

The man directed me upstairs, saying I would see the sign as soon as I got up there.

The wooden stairs were narrow and slightly tilted. I wondered if they had always been like that, or if the building had settled over the years, causing the entire stairwell to shift. It made me feel a bit dizzy, and when I reached the top of the stairs, I paused to let my equilibrium right itself.

The sign for the classifieds desk was, as the man had promised, right in front of me. As I gazed around the room, though, I spotted Ross Banning. I immediately thought of his exposé about Ella's boyfriend, and his hints that either Ella or Kyle could have been responsible for Wynn's death. And, of course, I couldn't forget what he had said about me meeting secretly with Jeff and Claw.

I felt my anger about the article flare up again, and before I could stop them, my feet started heading toward Ross's desk. *Don't do this,* I lectured myself. *Mama has probably written that letter to the editor already, and you're not going to help the situation.*

But it was like I was on autopilot. Ross didn't look up until I was right in front of his desk, and his initial smile of surprise quickly turned cautious. It must have been my frown and my crossed arms that put him on his guard.

"Is that why you were asking me questions about Ella?" I spat. "You wanted to find out if there was anything scandalous you could write about to make her look guilty?"

Ross crossed his arms, too, and stared at me. "I was looking for information, good or bad. What I found was bad, so I went with it."

"How could you? Ella didn't kill Wynn, and neither did Kyle."

The man at the desk nearest us stood and took a few steps toward me, but Ross waved him off. "It's fine," he told the man. "I can handle this." When Ross returned his attention to me, he said, "I don't like it, either, Olivia. Everyone, including you, talks about what a sweet girl Ella is. However, not a single one of us can deny she was caught on video going into the diner around the time the victim is believed to have been killed."

"That doesn't mean she did it," I said sullenly.

"My job is to find facts and present them to our readers," Ross said. "That's what I did, and I'm not going to apologize for it."

I let my eyes rove across the desk as I told myself to calm down. Making a scene in the middle of the newspaper office wasn't going to undo the damage that article had already done to Ella and Kyle. My gaze landed on a framed photo of an attractive couple who looked to be in their thirties. A boy who was probably seven or eight years old was between them, one hand in each of theirs. They were standing in front of a mountain range, all smiling happily at the camera.

"Truth or Consequences," I mumbled. It was written on the boy's T-shirt in large letters.

"It's a town," Ross said. "In New Mexico, south of Albuquerque. My sister and her family live there."

I looked closer at the photo. The sister didn't look

169

much like Ross in her face, with the exception of her eyes. She and Ross had the same shade of hazel eyes.

Exactly the same.

I felt both fear and sympathy welling up inside me. "Oh, Ross. That's you in the photo. You're the shifter. Hunters came for your family, didn't they?"

CHAPTER TWENTY-FIVE

Ross's eyes widened, just for a split second, and he jerked backward ever so slightly in his chair. He quickly hid his surprise, though, his face returning to a neutral expression. "What are you talking about?"

"That's not your sister," I said, pointing at the photo. "That's you." There was a tightness in my chest, and I felt slightly lightheaded. Ross had already killed Wynn, and I expected I had just leap-frogged over Claw to take the number one spot on his list of who to kill next.

It's okay. You're in a room full of people. He won't try anything right now.

Even though I was counting on the other people in the newsroom to provide some measure of safety for me, that didn't mean I wanted them to hear what Ross and I were discussing. I said in a low voice, "Did you kill Wynn for revenge? Did he come after your family?"

Ross bit his lip. I jumped when he suddenly reached forward, but he wasn't trying to get to me. Instead, he picked up the photo frame and pulled it toward him. He put his finger against the glass. "Wynn didn't kill my family. His father did."

"Brandon."

"He thought I was Jake, my husband. Brandon believed a shapeshifter in the form of a man had married a normal woman and had a son with her, but it was the opposite. I was Alyssa, and Jake was normal. I came home one day and found both Jake and my son…" Ross broke off and turned his head away.

"I'm so sorry, Ross." I meant it, too. Even a killer didn't deserve to lose his family like that.

"The hunter didn't want a monster having babies."

"You lived not too far from Albuquerque, so I'm guessing you already had connections that made it easy for you to learn about Kyle's police record there, as well as the outstanding warrant for Wynn's arrest."

"I was a journalist there. After… After what happened to my family, I came to Nightmare. I had heard rumors about Baxter Shackleford's collection of monsters, and even though I didn't want to be one of his pets, I figured Nightmare must be relatively safe if they could all survive here."

Ross looked at me pleadingly. "I intended to live a quiet life. Then, one day, Jeff showed up. He was known to be a ruthless hunter. I watched him closely, but he seemed to be truly retired from hunting. So, I calmed down and stopped worrying about it. Then Wynn arrived. He looked just like his father."

"Did you kill Brandon, too?"

Ross gave a short nod. "They never caught me, but I got my revenge. Or I thought I had, at least. But when I realized that hunter had a kid, I saw the chance to get true closure for my family. If my son couldn't live, then neither could the hunter's."

"You wrote in that article that I had been seen with Jeff and Claw, having a secret meeting at the campground. You were the camper who walked past us, weren't you? The woman with the water bottle. You were spying on us."

"I wanted to know if the hunters were onto me. When I killed the hunter who ruined my life, I took his notebook, but there wasn't much in there about my kind. I had hoped Jeff and Claw wouldn't realize what I was."

"Ross, you're going to have to confess to the police. You can't let Ella take the blame. It will ruin her life."

Ross stood slowly. "You're right. It will ruin her life. But I won't let anyone punish me for doing what was right, for getting justice for my family."

On that last word, Ross threw the framed photo at me. I instinctively reached out to catch it, and when I glanced up again, he was making a run for it toward a door at the back of the room.

"Stop!" I yelled. "He killed Wynn! Call the police!"

I knew, though, that by the time the police arrived, it would be too late. Ross would be someone else, and no one would ever find him. He would blend in with all the tourists out on High Noon Boulevard, and he would slip out of Nightmare to start a new life in a new body somewhere else.

So I started running. The door Ross had gone through led to another stairwell, and I could hear him clattering down the steps when I burst through the door. By the time I got to the ground floor, the door there was already closing. I wrenched it open and paused as sunlight flooded my vision. I was outside.

I blinked, and my eyes adjusted to the brightness, but I didn't see Ross. Then, I heard yelling to my right. I dashed to the edge of the building and turned the corner to see Ross on the ground with Cowan on top of him, right in the middle of the dirt street. Jeff was holding a small cast-iron skillet over Ross's head.

With his free hand, Jeff pulled his cell phone out of his pocket and started punching the screen with his thumb. "Got him for you, Olivia!" he shouted gleefully.

"How did you know he was the killer?" I asked breathlessly. That run down the stairs had been more cardio than I was prepared for.

"Why else would someone be running out of the building like their life depended on it?" Cowan asked. "Besides, he was trying to shift while he fled, which means he wasn't giving the change his full concentration. It went a little sideways for him."

Cowan gestured at Ross, and I recoiled when I saw the side of his face that wasn't pressed into the dirt. It had a slightly melted appearance. It looked like Ross had tried to shift into a different person, but he had failed to complete the process.

"Yuck," I said under my breath. To Cowan, I said, "How did you know to come here in the first place?"

"Our timing was just good luck. We were actually on our way to the library. Claw texted Jeff, saying he was going there to make copies, and that he could use some help putting up flyers."

"Guess my help wasn't enough." I thought it was odd Claw hadn't mentioned he would be bringing Cowan and Jeff into the plan, though I didn't care if they knew. Their help would have made putting up flyers go a lot faster.

Jeff had been talking quickly into his phone while still brandishing the skillet at Ross. I recognized it as the type of skillet the diner used to serve fajitas. Despite its diminutive size, I knew it could be detrimental to Ross. "The police are on their way," Jeff said, putting his phone back into his pocket. He was grinning, but rather than looking happy, he looked sinister as he leaned down closer to Ross. "And if you don't return to the form of Ross Banning, I'll be happy to shove this skillet into your face."

Ross struggled against Cowan's grip, and Cowan answered by shifting so he had one knee firmly on Ross's back. I could see the moment Ross gave up. His body suddenly sagged, and he let out a moan. As I watched, his face began to morph. It lost the melted look, and he soon appeared normal again.

"It won't last," Ross said in a quiet but confident voice. "All I have to do is take on the form of a prison guard, and I'll be gone before they even realize I'm missing."

"We could take care of him ourselves," Cowan suggested. To emphasize his point, he leaned more weight onto his knee.

"No," Jeff said firmly. "I left the hunter life. We're doing it the proper way, the legal way. However, if this shapeshifter is stupid enough to come back to Nightmare, then I'll let you do whatever you like to him."

Cowan smiled. "I hope he's stupid."

"Before you two make me a witness to your own murder plans," I said, "let's talk about Ella. Even if Ross admits to killing Wynn, that doesn't change the fact it looks like Ella who went into the diner that night."

"Ross is going to tell the police he doctored the video," Jeff said. "It's not far from the truth, is it, Ross?"

"The kid was stalking her. It made sense to frame her," Ross said. There was anger in his voice, but no trace of remorse for framing an innocent woman. "I had been to The Lusty enough to know where the cameras were, so I made sure her face showed up that night. I made it look like she was sleepwalking, so the police wouldn't get suspicious when she denied any memory of it."

I heard sirens and knew the police were close. It's not like they had far to drive since the police station was just a few streets over. If there was anything I wanted to know, then I needed to ask it immediately. "Ross, why was Wynn at the diner at three in the morning, anyway? How did you get him there?"

"He thought he was following Ella home that night, but it was actually me. I told him I'd meet him at The Lusty later if he would leave me alone until then. I knew the back door of the diner could be shimmied open, so I unlocked it and waited for Wynn to show up." Ross chuckled, apparently pleased with his cunning. "There's no security camera back there."

That explained why Wynn was never caught on camera that night. "Did he realize it wasn't actually Ella he was meeting?" I asked.

"I told him the truth, somewhere between stabbing him and drowning him." Ross's bravado faltered. "But there was something wrong with him. Something off. He fought back with more strength than I would have expected."

"He had been bitten by a ghoul. He was turning," Jeff said. "I was trying to help the kid."

"He got what he deserved," Ross grumbled.

"And you're about to get what you deserve." Cowan looked at Jeff. "I'm a stranger in this town, and I don't want to get wrapped up in a murder investigation. I'm going to take off."

Jeff smiled. "I'll tell the police I did the apprehending all by myself. They'll call me a hero in the newspaper, and business at The Lusty will boom because of it."

Cowan was already up and moving, and he disappeared around the corner of the newspaper building just as a police car turned onto the street. Ross started talking as soon as the two officers were out of the car, telling them he was the one who had killed Wynn and framed Ella. In just a few minutes, Ross was on his feet and in handcuffs.

I was relieved to have the whole thing over with, and I took in a deep breath as I watched Ross slide into the backseat of the patrol car. I was also relieved the officers were two people I had never met. I could only imagine how Officer Reyes and Officer Wilkins would have reacted to finding me, yet again, right in the middle of the drama.

Not surprisingly, I was told I would have to go to the

station, along with Jeff, to give a statement. We both agreed and said we would walk over together. I was certain Jeff was thinking the same thing I was: we could use the time during the walk to get our stories straight. That way, we could present a narrative to the police that didn't involve the supernatural or Cowan.

First, though, I wanted to check on Claw. He was surely done with printing off copies of the flyer, and I was surprised he hadn't come running when he heard the commotion. The police sirens, at least, should have gotten his attention.

Jeff and I went inside the library, but there was no sign of Claw. There was also no answer when Jeff tried calling him. I knew nothing bad had happened to him since his attacker was in custody, so I tried to fight the rising dread I felt about his disappearance.

We were halfway to the police station when I heard a phone ringing. "Oh, that must be Claw. Answer it!" I said to Jeff.

"That's not my ringtone."

I had totally forgotten about Baxter's cell phone. The trilling was, in fact, coming from my purse, and I hurried to fish the phone out so I could answer before it went to voicemail.

Damien didn't bother to identify himself when I answered, but I knew it was him. His voice was shaking, and I could hear his anger. "Are you with those hunters?"

"I'm with Jeff, the owner of The Lusty. Cowan just left, and we caught Wynn's killer."

"Tell Jeff to come pick up his trash."

"Um, excuse me? What are you talking about, Damien?"

"We just caught Claw trying to sneak into the Sanctuary."

CHAPTER TWENTY-SIX

I shut my eyes and pinched the ridge of my nose. Unfortunately, I didn't stop walking before I did that, and I stumbled over a stone on the sidewalk. When a noise of surprise escaped my lips, Damien immediately asked, "Are you in danger?"

"No, I'm just a klutz. Why on earth is Claw at the Sanctuary? He was supposed to be making copies at the library!"

"He says he woke up this morning with a hunch the shapeshifter was hiding out here, disguised as one of the employees. Sound familiar? He only wanted you to think he was working on the yard sale plan. As soon as you turned your back, he raced here."

"What was he going to do, go from bed to bed and put a piece of iron against everyone?" I shivered at the idea of my friends sleeping inside the Sanctuary while a hunter was roaming its halls. Jeff stopped walking and turned to me with wide eyes, listening intently to my side of the conversation, and I realized Claw had asked him and Cowan to go to the library to ensure they were nowhere near the Sanctuary. Claw had rounded up those of us who might have stopped him.

Damien was quiet for a moment, and when he spoke again, I could sense how hard he was trying to control his anger. "He was going to start with Madge, because Cowan told him about their history."

No wonder Damien was riled up. He was only running the Sanctuary because he felt like it was his duty in the wake of his dad's disappearance, but he took the job—and the safety of his employees—seriously. I felt my own anger rising, and I wanted to tell Damien to call the police and have Claw arrested for trespassing.

But then what? He would eventually be freed, and neither Claw nor Damien could tell the police the real reason for his presence at the Sanctuary.

"Claw's best friend was horribly killed just a week ago," I said, looking at Jeff's anxious face. "And Jeff already lost both his own best friend and that friend's son. Please don't make it any worse for him, or for Claw."

"You're asking me to just let him go?" Damien growled.

"I'm asking you to show him compassion. Feel free to threaten him, so he never considers coming to the Sanctuary again, but don't hurt him, please."

"Fine." Damien spat out the word.

"Jeff and I are on our way to the police station to give our statements. I'll head to the Sanctuary as soon as I'm done."

"Statements?"

"I just told you we caught Wynn's killer."

Damien laughed self-consciously. "I wasn't really listening."

"To be fair, you're dealing with your own drama. I'll see you soon." I hung up the phone and immediately repeated the conversation to Jeff. He had relaxed a bit when he heard me asking Damien not to hurt Claw, but he still seemed worried.

"It was a stupid thing for him to do. I'm sorry I

brought this on all of you, and on Ella," Jeff said when I had finished.

"Wynn came here looking for help. None of this is your fault."

I called Mama before putting away my phone. I wanted her to know that not only was I safe, but so was she. There was no need for her to worry about Cowan anymore. Mama was shocked to know Cowan had helped catch Wynn's killer, but she was more relieved than anything.

Jeff and I reached the front door of the police station just as Ella walked out of it. She had a dazed look on her face, but when she saw me, she dashed forward and wrapped her arms around me in a tight hug. "They let me go!" she cried. "Can you believe I was framed by that guy from the newspaper?"

"I can believe it," I said.

"But why would he have wanted Wynn dead? It makes no sense." Ella released me and gave Jeff a hug.

Ella was right. Ross would have to come up with some reason for killing Wynn that didn't involve monster hunters or the fact he was a shapeshifter. That wasn't my problem, though. All I cared about was that the real killer was behind bars, and Ella was free.

By the time I was finished at the police station, it was already midafternoon. I had walked to The Caffeinated Cadaver to meet Claw, and instead of walking back to the motel to retrieve my car, I walked to the Sanctuary. I was getting a lot of exercise chasing criminals around Nightmare.

I found Zach standing at the front doors, his knees slightly bent and his shoulders rounded. He was clearly on high alert and ready for trouble. "It's just me," I called as I approached, even though that was pretty obvious.

Zach's stance only relaxed slightly. "I caught him climbing through a window around back."

"It's a good thing you did. I'm glad you're here to keep everyone safe."

Zach made a guttural noise. "Catching him was a lot more satisfying than selling tickets every night. Too bad life has to return to normal and boring now."

Leave it to Zach to find something to be grumpy about, when he should have been celebrating the day as a win. The killer had been caught, Zach had prevented Claw from doing any harm, and Ella was free. It had been a good day.

Zach told me I would find Damien in his office, but when I went inside the building, he was just coming out of the entrance to the west wing, where the haunt started. "Where's Claw?" I asked.

"Gone. I doubt you'll see Cowan at the motel, either. I'm guessing both of them are already on the Interstate. After we caught Claw here, I sent Malcolm to the motel to let Cowan know he needed to get himself and Claw out of Nightmare before our compassion ran out."

"I appreciate you not killing him."

"We're not the monsters," Damien said firmly. He drew in a deep breath and let it out slowly. "We need to talk. Come on."

Damien turned and headed back into the haunt, and I followed. The overhead lights were on, so it was easy to see and a lot less spooky. Damien didn't stop until we were in the scene that looked like a forest. It was where the witches huddled around a giant cauldron each night. Usually, the branches of the fake trees looked like they were glowing in moonlight, but with the overhead lights on, it felt like we were standing in a clearing on a sunny day.

"Why are we in here?" I asked, looking around.

"For privacy."

I wanted to point out we could have had privacy in Damien's office, but if he wanted to chat in a fake forest, then who was I to argue? "What do you want to talk about that's so secret?"

"I'm sure you've figured it out by now."

I narrowed my eyes and looked closely at Damien. Was I missing something obvious? "Figured out what?"

"The truth about me."

I thought back over our conversations during the past few weeks. I knew a lot of truths about Damien. He hadn't wanted to come back to Nightmare. He didn't like the Sanctuary or the people who lived and worked there. He had a chip on his shoulder that was the size of a boulder, and he seemed to blame his dad for a lot of that.

His dad. This was about Baxter. I should have realized it in the moment, but so much had been going on that it had sailed right over my head. "You said you don't know what kind of supernatural creature your dad is," I said. "That means you don't know what you are."

Damien nodded. I thought of his green eyes, which flashed when he was feeling heightened emotions. I wondered how terrifying it was for Damien to know he had some kind of power without understanding what it was or what he was capable of.

"What about your mother? What was she?"

"I never knew my mother." Damien reached out and touched the necklace he had given me for protection. His fingers felt warm against my skin. "This is all I have of hers, and my father refused to speak of her. For all I know, she wasn't supernatural, and I'm half human."

"I assume you've explored your abilities to try to figure out what you are."

"I didn't think I was anything. Then, in high school, I got in a fight, and I felt this electricity surge through me. My supernatural abilities were waking up. When I told my father, he instantly started teaching me to control them. He was worried I could be dangerous. I was taught that my abilities were a curse, not a gift."

No wonder Damien has issues with his dad and everyone at the Sanctuary. As long as Damien was there, he was surrounded by people who not only knew what they were, but they were proud of it. They got to show off their supernatural side every night for the tourists, while Damien was scared and confused. Everyone spoke so highly of Baxter, and I wondered what had happened to make him treat his own son that way. Surely, he had known it would make Damien resentful.

I wasn't even sure what to say. At the moment, all I could think was how awful life must have been for Damien from the moment he knew he was supernatural. Mama and Madge had both implied Damien's dislike of the Sanctuary had involved Baxter somehow, and this had to be the source of his ire. I couldn't believe I was feeling pity for Damien. Suddenly, his jerk attitude made sense, and I wanted to hug him close and tell him it was going to be okay, but we were definitely not at that point in our relationship.

I continued to stand there in stunned silence, and Damien finally said, "Whether your conjuring skills are a gift or a curse is up to you. I can teach you how to control your ability, so you don't become dangerous."

"You'll use the same techniques Baxter did, right? But he didn't teach you to control your abilities. He taught you to hide them and pretend they didn't exist."

"The concept is still the same. I accused you of wanting Wynn to stop harassing Ella so badly that it resulted in his death. I was wrong to say that. The fact remains, though, that a conjuror can be dangerous if they can't control their ability. I want you to be safe, and that includes being safe from yourself."

I shifted awkwardly and turned to gaze at the trunk of a nearby tree. "I still think I'm just a regular-old human."

"I think you're a lot more than that. Please, Olivia. I may not like my father, but I do want to find him. You heard his voice for a reason. I truly believe that. If you let me help you, we might have a better chance of bringing him home."

That plea was a lot more effective at getting me to agree to Damien's proposal. And, I told myself, if I didn't have any supernatural abilities to begin with, then working on techniques to control them wouldn't do any harm. I nodded. "Okay. You can help me."

Damien smiled. "Good. We can start tomorrow."

A NOTE FROM THE AUTHOR

Thank you for reading *Drowning at the Diner*! I hope you're enjoying Olivia's continuing adventures in Nightmare as much as I am.

Before you go, would you please take a moment to leave a review for this book? As an indie author, reviews mean so much because they really do make a difference.

Eternally Yours,

Beth

P.S. You can keep up with my latest book news, get fun freebies, and more by signing up for my newsletter at Beth-Dolgner.com!

Slaying at the Saloon

NIGHTMARE, ARIZONA BOOK THREE
PARANORMAL COZY MYSTERIES

When a server is found with a stake through her heart onstage at Nightmare Saloon, everyone at Nightmare Sanctuary Haunted House worries a vampire hunter is in town. After all, the murder happened just before the curtain rose for Allie Nunes, a vampire singer traveling through Nightmare.

Olivia Kendrick and her friends at the Sanctuary must protect Allie and the other vampires, all while trying to find out who slayed the saloon girl. But as more details emerge, Olivia realizes the victim had a dark past and a lot of enemies. Tracking down the killer won't be easy.

While Olivia works to solve the case, she also has to guide the handsome, brooding Damien Shackleford through a shocking discovery about his missing father. Starting over at midlife wasn't supposed to be this hard, or this dangerous...

ACKNOWLEDGMENTS

Once I finish my first round of revisions, my manuscripts are sent to my wonderful test readers. Thank you to Alex, David, Kristine, Lisa, Mom, and Sabrina for your invaluable feedback! Lia at Your Best Book Editor and Trish at Blossoming Pages see the manuscript next, and I'm so grateful for their editing skills. Thank you to Jena at Book-Mojo for such gorgeous covers, formatting, and marketing.

ABOUT THE AUTHOR

Beth Dolgner writes paranormal fiction and nonfiction. Her interest in things that go bump in the night really took off on a trip to Savannah, Georgia, so it's fitting that her first series—Betty Boo, Ghost Hunter—takes place in that spooky city. Beth also writes paranormal nonfiction, including her first book, *Georgia Spirits and Specters*, which is a collection of Georgia ghost stories.

Beth and her husband, Ed, live in Tucson, Arizona, with their three cats. They're close enough to Tombstone that Beth can easily visit its Wild West street and watch staged shootouts, all in the name of research for the Nightmare, Arizona series.

Beth also enjoys giving presentations on Victorian death and mourning traditions as well as Victorian Spiritualism. She has been a volunteer at an historic cemetery, a ghost tour guide, and a paranormal investigator.

Keep up with Beth and sign up for her newsletter at BethDolgner.com.

BOOKS BY BETH DOLGNER

The Nightmare, Arizona Series
Paranormal Cozy Mystery
Homicide at the Haunted House
Drowning at the Diner
Slaying at the Saloon (September 2023)

The Eternal Rest Bed and Breakfast Series
Paranormal Cozy Mystery
Sweet Dreams
Late Checkout
Picture Perfect
Scenic Views
Breakfast Included
Groups Welcome
Quiet Nights

The Betty Boo, Ghost Hunter Series
Romantic Urban Fantasy
Ghost of a Threat
Ghost of a Whisper
Ghost of a Memory
Ghost of a Hope

Manifest
Young Adult Steampunk

A Talent for Death
Young Adult Urban Fantasy

Nonfiction
Georgia Spirits and Specters
Everyday Voodoo